A Dram of Drummhicit

Arthur Kopit
and Anton Dudley

A SAMUEL FRENCH ACTING EDITION

FOR PRODUCTION ENQUIRIES

UNITED STATES AND CANADA
Info@SamuelFrench.com
1-866-598-8449

UNITED KINGDOM AND EUROPE
Plays@SamuelFrench-London.co.uk
020-7255-4302

Each title is subject to availability from Samuel French, depending upon country of performance. Please be aware that *A DRAM OF DRUMMHICIT* may not be licensed by Samuel French in your territory. Professional and amateur producers should contact the nearest Samuel French office or licensing partner to verify availability.

*A **DRAM OF DRUMMHICIT*** was first produced by the La Jolla Playhouse, in San Diego, California on May 17, 2011. The production was directed by Christopher Ashley, with sets by David Zinn, costumes by David C. Woolard, lighting by Philip Rosenberg, sound by John Gromada, and projections by Tara Knight. The Production Stage Manager was Anjee Nero. The cast was as follows:

ROBERT BRUCE . . . . .Murphy Guyer

CHARLES PEARSE . . . . .Lucas Hall

WILLIAM ROSS . . . . Alan Mandell

HARRY MORGAN . . . . .Joseph Culliton

MACKENZIE STEWART . . . . .Kelly AuCoin

FIONA . . . . Polly Lee

OLD ANGUS . . . . .John Ahlin

FELICITY OLIPHANT . . . . Kathryn Meisle

REVEREND HAGGLEHORNE . . . . Larry Paulson

LITTLE NICK . . . . .Daniel Rubiano

CHARACTERS

REVEREND THOMAS HAGGLEHORNE – minister of a small parish church on Muckle Skerry

LITTLE NICK – his sexton (late teens to 20s)

ROBERT BRUCE – an American real estate mogul (50s)

CHARLES PEARSE – Robert Bruce's "fixer" (early to mid 30s)

HARRY MORGAN – a wealthy Edinburgh businessman (50s)

WILLIAM ROSS (a.k.a., Old Willy) – a resident of Muckle Skerry and business partner of Harry Morgan (70+)

MACKENZIE STEWART – owner of the only pub on Muckle Skerry (30s to 40s)

ANGUS MACLEOD (a.k.a., Old Angus) – a fisherman and frequenter of the pub (50s to 60s)

FIONA MACLEOD – the fisherman's daughter, works at the pub (early 20s)

FELICITY OLIPHANT – an anthropologist connected the British Museum (late 30s to 40s)

Various townsfolk

SETTING

The play takes place on Muckle Skerry, a small island somewhere in the Southern Hebrides, a few years back, when real estate investment still seemed like a good idea.

AUTHORS' NOTES

As far as we can tell, *A Dram of Drummhicit* is a romantic mystery/comedy/drama which touches on magic. This is why we never gave it a sub-title.

As a reader will soon discover, Muckle Skerry, the fictional Scottish island where this tale takes place, has many locales, including an old parish church, a charming local pub, a fisherman's hut (possibly haunted), an idyllic moor on the outskirts of town, and, looming down over the moor, a "forbidden hill." Clearly, literalism will get us nowhere.

And yet, like any play, if this story is to work, we must believe it all. Whatever lurks beneath the peaty soil of Muckle Skerry has to feel as real to us as it does to its inhabitants. Imagination is the key. This play is a journey to another world; judicious use of lights, sound, and minimal scenery – which together can *suggest* where we are rather than *tell* us where we are – are what will get us there.

– Arthur Kopit and Anton Dudley

Prologue

(Lights rise on a windswept, raid sodden island whose central monument is a lush green hill, the lower portion of which is visible in the background, the uppermost reaches out of sight.)

(Presently, we begin to hear people singing raucously, probably a traditional Scottish melody, lyrics in Gaelic – a classic "piobaireachd" or "big music" – accompanied by bagpipe.)

(Now the singers come into view. An odd celebration is clearly taking place as the celebrants' faces are all painted in bright colors and their bodies draped in vine leaves and flowers. Some seem to be wearing Druidic robes.)

(As they get closer, we also see that they are carrying someone aloft on their shoulders, which we'll come to know as the Green Man; a dark figure with carrot-red hair, its body decorated with garlands of wild flowers.)

(It begins to rain.)

(Undaunted, the celebrants head for town, a route that takes them past a small, lonely-looking parish church, where we notice a lone man watching through a window.)

(Some of the celebrants notice him as well, and wave.)

(The man does not wave back. Instead, he watches them pass from sight, song fading as they do.)

(The church glides forward, that man still at the window.)

(Then its walls swing open, and in we go.)

Scene 1

(Inside the church, that man we saw at the window, the **REVEREND THOMAS HAGGLEHORNE,** *late forties but aging rapidly, turns from the window and looks up.)*

REVEREND HAGGLEHORNE. *(looking up)* Really Lord, I mean it. Any parish but this one!

(sound of a car pulling up)

And I don't mean to press, but the sooner you can get me transferred, the better.

(He rushes to the door, takes a deep breath, then throws it open, huge smile on his face, as if nothing were wrong.)

Hello! Hello!

(sound of car doors shutting)

Come in, come in!

(Enter, in a rush, three **MEN,** *all drenched from rain. In the distance, a rumble of thunder can be heard.)*

(The first one in is the church sexton, a young man known as **LITTLE NICK,** *carrying an umbrella that's too small to protect anyone. Making matters worse, it's just blown inside out.)*

(The other two men are **HARRY MORGAN,** *around 50, an Edinburgh businessman who looks prosperous even when wet, and an American,* **CHARLES PEARSE,** *early 30s, instantly likable, with an unmistakable aura of authority, a feeling reinforced by the small, bulky aluminum briefcase he carries in his left hand. The moment they enter...)*

LITTLE NICK. My God, this fuckin' rain, it just don't let up. And then the fuckin' *wind.* And the *COWS!* I mean there I am, drivin' back with these two when suddenly the wind is knockin' down all these cows, and one of 'em, I swear, is lifted straight up and flyin' straight toward the car!

REVEREND HAGGLEHORNE. Really!

LITTLE NICK. But luckily I swerved.

REVEREND HAGGLEHORNE. Well that's good news.

LITTLE NICK. Not that I'm blamin' our tardiness on a cow!

REVEREND HAGGLEHORNE. No-no, really, it's fine.

LITTLE NICK. Because that cow was nothin' compared to their *planes* comin' in! I mean they almost fuckin' crashed!

REVEREND HAGGLEHORNE. Yes, but what's important here is that they *didn't.* Did you?

HARRY MORGAN. What?

REVEREND HAGGLEHORNE. Crash.

HARRY MORGAN & CHARLES. *(together)* No.

LITTLE NICK. Yes but they *almost* did! I say if you gotta fly, do so in somethin' *big,* so if ya crash you've at least got some *support.*

REVEREND HAGGLEHORNE. That is an excellent point.

LITTLE NICK. No, big planes is the ticket!

HARRY MORGAN. And from now on, we will try to fly in big ones only.

LITTLE NICK. There ya go!

REVEREND HAGGLEHORNE. This has been very sound advice.

LITTLE NICK. But the worst of all –

REVEREND HAGGLEHORNE. Nick, do us a favor, would you? Before you say another word, *think.* And then try not to.

(**LITTLE NICK,** *who was about to say more, stops and thinks. With great effort, he manages not to say it.*)

Mr. Morgan, good to see you again. I gather your flight was a bit turbulent.

HARRY MORGAN. We are here, let us just leave it at that.

REVEREND HAGGLEHORNE. Good. Yes. And you must be Charles. I've heard so much about you. The Reverend Thomas Hagglehorne, at your service.

(*They shake hands. As they do,* **REVEREND HAGGLEHORNE** *notices the aluminum case* **CHARLES** *is holding.*)

Nick, come on, take this from the man, what is wrong with you?

LITTLE NICK. I can't.

(**REVEREND HAGGLEHORNE** *looks closer, and sees that the case is actually connected to* **CHARLES**' *wrist by a chain. For the first time, we see the chain, too.*)

REVEREND HAGGLEHORNE. Oh…yes. Right…is this all you brought?

LITTLE NICK. No, the rest of his stuff's still in the boot. I thought it best if we first ascertained where he was stayin', and then brought it there.

REVEREND HAGGLEHORNE. Yes. Good thinking, Nick. Actually, I'm not sure they've determined that as yet. We weren't expecting you for a few more days.

CHARLES. I know. Sorry about that. But in situations that demand my presence, such as this one here, Mr. Bruce likes me to arrive a few days ahead of schedule, believing that catching people off-guard provides a more accurate picture of what's actually going on. And sometimes that's true, and sometimes it's not, but that's what he likes, so that's what I do.

REVEREND HAGGLEHORNE. Makes perfect sense.

CHARLES. So where are the bodies now?

REVEREND HAGGLEHORNE. In the back room.

LITTLE NICK. No they're not.

REVEREND HAGGLEHORNE. That's right, no they're not. Nick moved 'em out last night.

LITTLE NICK. I thought it would be safer if we stored 'em in the cellar.

REVEREND HAGGLEHORNE. That's 'cause in back there are all these windows, so it's not hard to get in if you're so inclined. And some people around here –

LITTLE NICK. Not just some.

REVEREND HAGGLEHORNE. No, Nick's right, it's the whole bloody town. They want to put the bodies back in the ground, ya see. Where they were.

LITTLE NICK. And for fuckin' centuries, too!

REVEREND HAGGLEHORNE. Yes, well, in a manner of speaking.

LITTLE NICK. It's our sacred fuckin' duty!

REVEREND HAGGLEHORNE. Nick and I have differing views on this, but there is truth in what he says. Still, as a Christian, and a man of God, I consider it my godly duty to give these poor souls a proper Christian burial.

LITTLE NICK. But they are PRE-Christian! *PRE!* Why can you not understand that?

REVEREND HAGGLEHORNE. Well I do. And they are indeed pre-Christian. But surely that was not their fault.

LITTLE NICK. That is not the fucking point!

CHARLES. I'm sorry, but could we hold this discussion off for just a bit? Obviously it's a crucial one. But just for now. Till we're up to speed on this.

REVEREND HAGGLEHORNE. That's right. You listen t' him now. He's Mr. *Bruce's* man! And without him none o' this would be happening! *(to* **CHARLES***)* Am I not right?

CHARLES. Absolutely.

REVEREND HAGGLEHORNE. So would you like some tea?

CHARLES. I'd love some, thank you

HARRY MORGAN. Me as well.

REVEREND HAGGLEHORNE. If ya don't mind, Nick, get our guests some tea.

LITTLE NICK. Tea comin' up!

(exit, **LITTLE NICK***)*

REVEREND HAGGLEHORNE. The truth is – and please keep this t' yourselves – but from my particular perspective, it's nice to have a few folks here in the church, dead or not it at least helps fill the space.

(**HARRY MORGAN** *and* **CHARLES** *stare at him, startled*)

LITTLE NICK. *(offstage)* WHAT KIND O' TEA?

CHARLES. Oh, any kind.

HARRY MORGAN. Same here!

CHARLES. Do people not come for services?

REVEREND HAGGLEHORNE. Not as a rule, no.

LITTLE NICK. WHAT ABOUT MILK?

CHARLES. No milk.

HARRY MORGAN. Nor for me!

REVEREND HAGGLEHORNE. In fact, frankly, I can't recall anybody comin' even *once*. On the other hand, apparently no one came for my predecessors either. So this can't be my fault entirely… Actually, I misspoke just now. Yer friend, Mr. Ross, he's been comin' recently. Which makes me feel there may be some hope left.

CHARLES. I believe he was supposed to meet us here.

REVEREND HAGGLEHORNE. Oh yes! He sent word, he'll meet you at the pub. He's not been feelin' well of late.

LITTLE NICK. WHAT ABOUT CRACKERS?

REVEREND HAGGLEHORNE. We've never had crackers here, Nick, you know that!

LITTLE NICK. I could run down to the pub.

CHARLES. It's fine.

REVEREND HAGGLEHORNE. NO CRACKERS!

LITTLE NICK. NO CRACKERS COMIN' UP!

REVEREND HAGGLEHORNE. So what else d'ya want to know?

CHARLES. How many bodies are there?

REVEREND HAGGLEHORNE. As of this mornin' there was an even duzzen. Then it rained, and now there's twenty.

CHARLES. What's rain have to do with it?

REVEREND HAGGLEHORNE. Well the rain affects the soil ya see. And when it gets all saturated, it kind o' pinches in and out they pop, sort o' like a pimple, only bigger. It's an alarmin' sight. I've seen one and it's enough fer a lifetime. I was just out strollin' on the heath when, pop, there it was, at me feet, this grotesque head with ginger red hair.

HARRY MORGAN. Was that the first?

REVEREND HAGGLEHORNE. Oh no, this was after. The first was by Ballater Bay. Your construction crew found that one while layin' in a new access road. Then their backhoe dug up some more, so that ended construction. They're all over the place. And people do find 'em from time to time, just never in quite this quantity. The ones that came in since mornin' were found by some woman from the British Museum, Felicity somethin'-or-other.

HARRY MORGAN. Oliphant.

REVEREND HAGGLEHORNE. That's it. You've spoken to her, I guess.

CHARLES. We both have.

REVEREND HAGGLEHORNE. Well it's a sweet name she has, but she is definitely no sweetie-pie. No, she is one tough nut.

CHARLES. I'll need to meet with her as soon as I can.

REVEREND HAGGLEHORNE. And you will. She knows yer comin'. But, like all of us, was not expectin' you so soon. Speaking of which, I'm not sure what they have told you about accommodations, but the town doesn't have a proper hotel ya see. People don't come here as a rule. Though with this new golf course of yours, all that will definitely change.

CHARLES. Assuming we can get these bodies out.

REVEREND HAGGLEHORNE. Well that goes without sayin'. Playin' golf with bodies poppin' up is not a desirable feature on any course, even one with a lot o' hazards.

CHARLES. I'm sure we'll be able to take care of it.

REVEREND HAGGLEHORNE. I'm sure ya will too. HOW'S THE TEA CUMMIN' BY THE WAY?

LITTLE NICK. OKAY!

REVEREND HAGGLEHORNE. Water doesn't boil fast here.

LITTLE NICK. HAVE YOU WARNED 'EM YET?

REVEREND HAGGLEHORNE. About…

LITTLE NICK. THE FLAVOR!

REVEREND HAGGLEHORNE. Oh yes, good idea. Frankly, the water here has got a bit of a *crunchy* feel. It's from the peat ya see, which infuses the water with a sort of mossy aftertaste. Plus somethin' else, which probably has to do with these Bog People bein' such an integral part of the saturated mix. Some people like the taste. And some don't.

CHARLES. I think maybe we'll skip the tea.

REVEREND HAGGLEHORNE. SKIP THE TEA!

LITTLE NICK. CANCELING TEA!

REVEREND HAGGLEHORNE. So, would you like to see the bodies?

CHARLES. That's why we're here.

REVEREND HAGGLEHORNE. Right-o. Nick, go get the keys to the cellar, I'll go find a candle. There's no light down there. But candlelight should be sufficient.

(*exit,* **REVEREND HAGGLEHORNE** *and* **LITTLE NICK**)

CHARLES. If Ross is not at the pub when we arrive, I want you to go get him.

HARRY MORGAN. He'll be there.

CHARLES. He'd better be. Ross should've known about all this. He *lives* here, for Chrissake!

HARRY MORGAN. Not full-time.

CHARLES. But full enough. This is inexcusable. You brought Mr. Bruce in on this, Harry. He *trusted* you. Do you know what that means?

HARRY MORGAN. Of course.

CHARLES. Actually, I don't think you do. Mr. Bruce is invested in this project, Harry, not just financially, but emotionally. *Emotionally.*

HARRY MORGAN. I understand.

CHARLES. Again, I don't think you do, so please don't say that if you don't. As for this little problem here, I will handle it. What I am *concerned* about is what this suggests about our Scottish partnership, which includes Mr. Ross. This is *your* team, Harry.

HARRY MORGAN. I will take care if it.

CHARLES. I know you will.

(**REVEREND HAGGLEHORNE** *reappears with a candle.*)

Now. Let's go see those bodies…

REVEREND HAGGLEHORNE. Before we do, I think we should prepare you. They are of course mummies, and a bit startling when one sees 'em for the first time.

LITTLE NICK. Or the second.

REVEREND HAGGLEHORNE. Or indeed any time.

LITTLE NICK. Very startling indeed.

REVEREND HAGGLEHORNE. And that's not just because they are so perfectly preserved, though they are. But because…*well…*

LITTLE NICK. Because they all have nooses around their necks.

REVEREND HAGGLEHORNE. And we're not sure what that means.

(*And with that, the* **REVEREND HAGGLEHORNE** *and* **LITTLE NICK** *lead the two men down a corridor, candle lighting the way. Vague sound of thunder is in the distance.*)

Scene 2

*(The Pub. At rise, **CHARLES** is at a table with **FELICITY OLIPHANT**, an archaeologist connected to the British Museum, and dressed for serious trekking. Both are drinking beer.)*

*(As they do, activity goes on quietly behind them. Some kind of secret celebration is being organized, and the pub master, **MACKENZIE STEWART**, is the leader.)*

*(Helping serve drinks is **FIONA MACLEOD**, a waitress in her early 20s with fiery red hair. Among the others in the pub is her father, **ANGUS MACLEOD**, known to all as **OLD ANGUS**.)*

FELICITY. Generally, they're referred to as bog bodies, or bog people. The reason they look the way they do is from the tannins in the soil. And because there's no oxygen in the bog, they don't decompose. Which is what makes them so valuable. I mean, we know so little about the Iron Age, so when something like this comes along –

*(**HARRY MORGAN** rushes in from another room.)*

HARRY MORGAN. *(to **FELICITY**)* Excuse me. *(to **CHARLES**)* Ross isn't here. *(back to **FELICITY**)* Sorry. Harry Morgan. We talked when all this…

FELICITY. Oh yes! Pleased to meet you.

HARRY MORGAN. What would you like me to do?

CHARLES. Find him.

HARRY MORGAN. Right. *(**HARRY MORGAN** thinks a moment. Then he gets an idea.)* Nice to meet you. *(He rushes out of the pub.)*

CHARLES. Sorry. You were saying…

FELICITY. Well! …just that when something like this occurs, it's like a kind of window has just opened, and suddenly one can see into a world that would otherwise be completely obscure. Who were these people? We don't really know.

CHARLES. Yes, well just so long as we get them out.

FELICITY. Ah, yes, but to where?

CHARLES. How about the British Museum?

FELICITY. Well that would indeed be wonderful…except –

CHARLES. It would cost a lot. No, I'm sure. And I have been officially authorized by Mr. Bruce to pay whatever it takes to get them from here to there.

FELICITY. …well that is quite an offer.

CHARLES. And if it requires building a new wing to house them, Mr. Bruce is willing to do that as well.

FELICITY. Well this is an extremely interesting piece of news. I'll need to think that over.

CHARLES. Of course. Just try not to take too long. We've got a bit of a schedule problem here.

(**FIONA** *stops by the table.*)

FIONA. Have you decided yet?

CHARLES. What?

FIONA. The menu. What you'd like to eat.

CHARLES. Ah. Yes. I think I'll try the "wood-smoked haddock."

FIONA. We're out of haddock.

CHARLES. What about the cod?

FIONA. Out of cod.

CHARLES. Mackerel?

FIONA. No mackerel.

CHARLES. Well have you got *any* fish?

FIONA. *(shouting to an old man at the bar)* DAD, DIDDYA CATCH ANY FISH TODAY?

OLD ANGUS. NO FISH TODAY!

FIONA. No fish today.

OLD ANGUS. BUT I DID CATCH SOME EELS OVER BY GILSENNY BAY, AND IF YOU'D LIKE I COULD SPARE ONE OR TWO!

CHARLES. I think not.

FIONA. NO THANKS, DAD!

OLD ANGUS. ANYTIME!

FIONA. How about some haggis?

CHARLES. I'm not a big fan of haggis.

FIONA. Well then ya wouldn't like this.

CHARLES. What's left?

FIONA. Mutton.

CHARLES. I'll try the mutton.

FIONA. And would ya like that with bashed neeps or champit tatties?

CHARLES. I have no idea what you just said.

FELICITY. Take the bashed neeps.

CHARLES. I'll go with the neeps.

FIONA. Bashed neeps it is!

(She leaves.)

CHARLES. Tell me about the nooses.

FELICITY. Oh yes. That is an eerie touch. No one's quite sure what it signifies. But I think it's part of some pagan ritual, most likely involving sacrifice. And *yet...*

How do you hang someone in a bog? It's too dense, gravity doesn't work the same. You don't drop down, you sink *slowly*, like passing from consciousness into a dream, if you see what I mean. No, those ropes wouldn't have worked if all they wanted was to kill these people. No-no, something else was going on. But *what?*

CHARLES. We're planning to build a golf course here.

FELICITY. I know. That could be a bit problematic now. I mean, there you are, in a sand-trap, and you see what you think is your ball, buried just a bit, so you take your swing, *and...*

CHARLES. Yes, thank you.

FELICITY. Not a happy thought.

CHARLES. No.

FELICITY. So you need to get the bodies out. Well I can certainly identify with that. To getting the bodies out!

CHARLES. To getting the bodies out!

(*They clink glasses and are about to drink when* **MACKENZIE STEWART** *raises a champagne bottle.*)

MACKENZIE STEWART. We can do better than beer! Fiona my sweet, bring out the other bottles. French champagne. Genuine! And not something we normally imbibe in but we do today thanks to the largesse of Mr. Robert Bruce, who is gifting us with not only a four-star champion-level golf course, which this island desperately needs...

(*cheers from the throng*)

...and his illustrious name to go with it, but has also sent us this man here as his personal representative. MR. CHARLES PEARSE, stand up please and accept our gratitude, and a rousin' Muckle Skerry cheer.

ALL. *Slàinte mhor! Slàinte gu soírraidh!*

MACKENZIE STEWART. Mr. Pearse, a few words if you would.

CHARLES. Well first, let me thank you all for your great hospitality.

MACKENZIE STEWART. Don't thank us for that yet. We're still tryin' to find you a proper place to stay.

CHARLES. If necessary I'll just stay here in this wonderful pub.

MACKENZIE STEWART. As many have, though seldom by choice. No, we can do better than that. I mean, we're not *totally* primitive here! So! Mr. Pearse, if you would...

CHARLES. Thank you. Well, to start with, I bring you Mr. Bruce's fondest wishes. As you probably already know, though some may not, Mr. Bruce visited here many years ago.

MACKENZIE STEWART. When he was a student!

CHARLES. That's correct.

SOMEONE IN THE PUB. In Glasgow!

MACKENZIE STEWART. No, Edinburgh! University o' Edinburgh! "Junior year abroad!" Am I right?

CHARLES. Absolutely right.

MACKENZIE STEWART. We know it all.

CHARLES. So then why am I telling you this?

MACKENZIE STEWART. Because we want to hear it from *American* lips. For all we know, maybe *you* don't have it right.

CHARLES. Well probably I don't.

MACKENZIE STEWART. Well then we will correct you. Proceed.

CHARLES. Well it was indeed his junior year abroad.

MACKENZIE STEWART. From where, what school? NAME THE SCHOOL!

CHARLES. Princeton.

MACKENZIE STEWART. That's correct. He was a Princetonian Tiger. Economics major. Wore a lot of orange, people say.

CHARLES. Sounds correct.

MACKENZIE STEWART. *Is* correct!

CHARLES. So one day, not sure how, he heard about this little island here.

MACKENZIE STEWART. He heard about it 'cause there's no other place like it, and sooner or later, word spreads!

CHARLES. Well that may be it.

MACKENZIE STEWART. Of course that's it.

CHARLES. So he borrowed his roommate's car.

MACKENZIE STEWART. And that roommate's name *was…*

CHARLES. Harry Morgan.

MACKENZIE STEWART. HARRY MORGAN! CORRECT AGAIN! And what kind o' car was it that Harry had?

CHARLES. I don't know.

MACKENZIE STEWART. It was a Morgan.

CHARLES. And was that because…

MACKENZIE STEWART. His family owned the fucking company.

CHARLES. Well now I know something else. So! Young Robert borrowed Harry Morgan's *Morgan,* and drove here. And though he spent only one day here –

MACKENZIE STEWART. ONLY ONE DAY HERE!

ALL THE OTHERS. ONLY ONE DAY HERE!

CHARLES. – that one day was for him not only the most wonderful, but *still* the only truly perfect day of his life.

MACKENZIE STEWART. I'll bet he was with a woman!

CHARLES. I suspect he was.

MACKENZIE STEWART. Of course he was. And I'll bet I know where they went when they got here.

CHARLES. He said it was a hill.

MACKENZIE STEWART. *We know the one! (to the others in the pub)* Don't we fellas?

VARIOUS MEN. WE DO INDEED!

CHARLES. And so, thanks to that one memorable visit, many years later, when Harry Morgan, who was now in real estate, came to him with a proposal for developing a major golf course on that very island, Mr. Bruce instantly said –

MACKENZIE STEWART. COUNT ME IN!

CHARLES. His very words.

ALL. COUNT ME IN!

MACKENZIE STEWART. To Robert the Bruce!

ALL. TO ROBERT THE BRUCE!

CHARLES. Whoa-whoa-whoa! He's not Robert the Bruce.

MACKENZIE STEWART. What d'ya mean?

CHARLES. I mean he's *Robert* Bruce. Not Robert *the* Bruce. Actually, I'm not even sure he's Scottish.

MACKENZIE STEWART. What's that got to do with it? Anyone named Robert Bruce is Scottish, and that's the end of it, and if ya don't agree you can get out now, and take yer bloody golf course with ya.

CHARLES. Well then I agree.

MACKENZIE STEWART. There ya go! *HE'S ONE OF US NOW!*

ALL . *HE'S ONE OF US NOW!*

MACKENZIE STEWART. And ya know what? Since he's now truly one o' us, that means he's a *real* man, and I say fuck this bubbling French shite. He deserves a MAN'S drink!

ALL. A *MAN'S* DRINK!

MACKENZIE STEWART. Fiona?

FIONA. Gettin' it.

MACKENZIE STEWART. You're about to make contact with what we are famous for! Our very own single-malt!

FIONA. *(returning with a bottle)* Here it is!

MACKENZIE STEWART. We'll start you out with just a little bit. Just a dram. Open please.

*(***FIONA*** opens the bottle.)*

And if you would now pour…

(She pours.)

And now we'll all take some…

(She pours them all a dram.)

To our new friend and honorary citizen of this fair town of Wormit, on the incomparable island of Muckle Skerry, we offer you a dram of Drummhicit!

CHARLES. Drum-*what?*

MACKENZIE STEWART. Drummhicit.

CHARLES. Drummhicit?

MACKENZIE STEWART. No, Drummhicit.

CHARLES. Drummhicit.

MACKENZIE STEWART. That's it.

CHARLES. DRUMMHICIT!

MACKENZIE STEWART. Ya just lost it.

CHARLES. Drummhicit.

MACKENZIE STEWART. There ya go!

(Note: To our ears, all these pronunciations should sound exactly the same.)

ALL. DRUMMHICIT!

*(But before **CHARLES** can drink, **MACKENZIE STEWART** stops him.)*

MACKENZIE STEWART. This little drink does require a chaser though. Have ya tasted our famous crunchy water yet?

CHARLES. No.

MACKENZIE STEWART. Get him some crunchy water. It's the perfect match. Without it, it's a bit of a challenge, though some do fancy it that way. The peppery, beyond smoky taste is the closest thing to eating a campfire that you'll ever do.

*(**FIONA** brings out a bottle of Muckle Skerry Crunchy Water.)*

We sell the water too. It's what you'd call a "specialty item." In fact, this and Drummhicit are our prime sources of income. Fishing used to be, but not lately. Still, it don't matter 'cause when that course is built, people will be comin' here in droves and payin' top dollar too, 'cause how many golf courses can you play on with bodies poppin' up?

CHARLES. …I'm not sure that's the way we want to go.

MACKENZIE STEWART. Well we'll leave this t' you. We're not the experts. We just know a good game when we see one. Anyway, to Mr. Pearse!

ALL. MR. PEARSE!

*(And now **CHARLES** drinks.)*

CHARLES. OH MY GOD! Oh my God, oh my God, oh my God… *(etc.)*

MACKENZIE STEWART. Quick, give him the crunchy water!

(They give the poor suffering man some crunchy water. He drinks it quickly. If anything it's even worse.)

CHARLES. *Oh my God...*

MACKENZIE STEWART. Some people like it, some don't.

CHARLES. *(barely able to speak)* This is unbelievable.

MACKENZIE STEWART. It's an acquired taste.

(enter, practically on the run, the **REVEREND HAGGLEHORNE, LITTLE NICK** *just behind him)*

REVEREND HAGGLEHORNE. All right, which o' you heathens did it? Which? Let's have it! 'Cause this is not right!

MACKENZIE STEWART. I don't know what you're talking about.

REVEREND HAGGLEHORNE. Sure ya do. There's a Bog Body missin'! Nick and I just did a head-count. And there were footsteps leading from our cellar door through the mud straight to here.

MACKENZIE STEWART. What would we do with a Bog Body?

REVEREND HAGGLEHORNE. How should I know? I only know not one o' you ever comes to church, and I think it's 'cause you're all pagans, the lot o' you! So what have ya done with that poor soul? Out with it! What's that over there?

MACKENZIE STEWART. What?

REVEREND HAGGLEHORNE. Behind that curtain. This wasn't here the other day. What's a curtain doin' in a pub?

(He yanks the curtain open. Behind it is an upright, extremely spooky looking bog body with blackened skin and ginger red hair, a noose around its neck, its arms splayed to the side, and being used as a coat rack.)

MACKENZIE STEWART. How the hell did this get here?

REVEREND HAGGLEHORNE. How indeed.

MACKENZIE STEWART. I mean that's just bloody disgustin'!

OLD ANGUS. And in a *pub* yet!

FIONA. Some people have no respect!

REVEREND HAGGLEHORNE. What's that in back?

MACKENZIE STEWART. What're you talkin' about?

REVEREND HAGGLEHORNE. In back. Behind this one. There's someone standin' there.

MACKENZIE STEWART. Why would someone do that?

REVEREND HAGGLEHORNE. No idea. Nick, move this one aside, would you?

(**LITTLE NICK** *goes to move the Bog Body aside. In so doing, he sees what's behind it, and stops short.*)

LITTLE NICK. You sure you wanna do this?

REVEREND HAGGLEHORNE. Of course I'm sure.

MACKENZIE STEWART. Fellas! Come, give the lad a hand. I'll help too. Little team-work. That's the way…

(**MACKENZIE STEWART** *and others leap into action. In the blur of activity,* **MACKENZIE STEWART** *manages to slip a greatcoat off the Bog-Body-As-Coat-Rack and drape it over what we now see is a* second *Bog Body, thus obscuring its body but not its head, which is festooned with leaves and flowers. We vaguely recognize the body as the one we saw being brought down the hill.*)

(*Note that there is also a noose around its neck, with a red rose adorning the noose's knot.*)

It's a bit cold in here, so we thought it best to keep 'm covered.

REVEREND HAGGLEHORNE. Did you?

MACKENZIE STEWART. On the other hand, maybe he'd be better off in back, near the oven. Fellas?

REVEREND HAGGLEHORNE. No, no. Please. I'm curious. Remove the coat, would you?

(**MACKENZIE STEWART** *lowers the coat half way*)

MACKENZIE STEWART. How's that?

(*Even the body's top half is spectacular, being wrapped from leathery head on down in vine leaves.*)

REVEREND HAGGLEHORNE. Lovely. Now the rest.

(**MACKENZIE STEWART** *removes the coat entirely, thereby revealing a prodigious phallus made from a tree branch bursting with flowers.*)

Oh my God…

MACKENZIE STEWART. I know. Can you believe it? The ol' man has sprouted!

OLD ANGUS. It must be spring!

REVEREND HAGGLEHORNE. Right. Where'd you get this one?

MACKENZIE STEWART. No idea.

SOMEONE ELSE. I think he just walked in.

REVEREND HAGGLEHORNE. Really? Funny, to me he looks like the one I saw you all carrying down the hill before.

MACKENZIE STEWART. So he does. You're right. Now I remember. That's it.

REVEREND HAGGLEHORNE. Right. Listen up. I want these two poor souls taken out o' here and put back where they rightfully belong, by which I mean the church.

MACKENZIE STEWART. Unfortunately, though we are all Scots, and therefore brave, I am not sure we're brave enough to enter a place like that.

REVEREND HAGGLEHORNE. Well one or more o' you were brave enough to break in and get that one out, and from the tracks on the ground and the mud on your shoes I'm guessing it was you, Mackenzie Stewart.

MACKENZIE STEWART. We had a desperate need of a coat rack.

REVEREND HAGGLEHORNE. And this one?

MACKENZIE STEWART. It's important to welcome spring in a vegetatively appropriate way, which, in our collective wisdom, we believed this was.

REVEREND HAGGLEHORNE. Well it's not.

MACKENZIE STEWART. Well ya see we didn't know that.

REVEREND HAGGLEHORNE. Maybe if ya went t' church now and then ya would.

MACKENZIE STEWART. Well now that's an interestin' idea. But frankly it feels a bit too radical.

OLD ANGUS. Don't forget the fish.

MACKENZIE STEWART. Thank you, Angus. Right you are. The fish! That's another reason.

REVEREND HAGGLEHORNE. For what?

ONE OF THE OTHERS. Makin' us a Green Man.

OLD ANGUS. Have ya noticed any fish lately? No you have not.

MACKENZIE STEWART. Well the Green Man has power!

OLD ANGUS. That he does.

MACKENZIE STEWART. And fish can feel it!

OLD ANGUS. That they can.

MACKENZIE STEWART. First clear day, you set this chap up by the water's edge, tie a string to his whatchmacallit – doesn't even need a worm, just a string! – and watch those fish start jumping.

REVEREND HAGGLEHORNE. Right.

(**LITTLE NICK** *finds a wheelbarrow in a side room*)

LITTLE NICK. We can use this!

REVEREND HAGGLEHORNE. Thank you, Nick. Now if some of you would please prop those two fellas up in here, my loyal sexton and I will take care o' this ourselves, thank you very much. Mr. Pearse, I can't imagine what you must be thinkin', but I for one am mightily embarrassed.

(*Led by* **MACKENZIE STEWART,** *they prop the two Bog People into the wheelbarrow. Exit,* **REVEREND HAGGLEHORNE** *and* **LITTLE NICK** *pushing the wheelbarrow, those two Bog People looking like some grotesque variation of zombie royalty.*)

MACKENZIE STEWART. Well that sure was a downer.

ONE OF THE OTHERS. Now where do we hang our coats?

MACKENZIE STEWART. You know what? Fuck the coats! We'll figure it out. DRINKS FOR ALL! We've got t' get back t' feelin' good again! Mr. Pearse, why don't ya help cheer us up even more and give us a hint of what's comin' down the pike from Mr. Robert the Bruce and his consortium of golf fanatics. Fer example: we know the general plan. But how exactly will the course be laid out?

CHARLES. Actually, we're still working on that.

MACKENZIE STEWART. Fair enough. Golf courses are tricky to design, we all know that. But how will it be *promoted?* That's somethin' people have been askin' me of late.

CHARLES. Right. Good question. Well initially we'll be stressing the island's proximity to Glasgow.

MACKENZIE STEWART. *What* proximity?

CHARLES. Approximately three and a half hours by car, I believe.

ONE OF THE OTHERS. In yer *dreams!*

MACKENZIE STEWART. Ya can't get here from Glasgow in under six!

SOMEONE ELSE. And then only if yer lucky!

CHARLES. Right. No-no, I understand. No, I'm talking about when the *bridge* is built.

MACKENZIE STEWART. *What* bridge?

OLD ANGUS. Old Willy said 'nothin' 'bout no fuckin' bridge.

CHARLES. Well you certainly can't expect a *ferry* to get all those people here.

MACKENZIE STEWART. SOMEONE GET OLD WILLY!

CHARLES. I believe Mr. Morgan has just gone for him.

(A general hubbub now breaks out.)

VARIOUS VOICES. *(voices overlapping)* Did Old Willy ever say anything to you about a bridge? / Not a word! / What will happen to our ferry? / I love that ferry! *(etc.)*

CHARLES. *(simultaneously)* All right, all right, calm down, calm down. WILL EVERYBODY PLEASE CALM DOWN!?

(They calm down.)

Obviously there's some confusion here. In your contracts...

MACKENZIE STEWART. *What* contracts?

CHARLES. The ones you signed.

OLD ANGUS. I signed no contract. Who here signed a contract?

ONE OF THE OTHERS. Not I!

SOMEONE ELSE. Not I!

A THIRD PERSON. Not I!

CHARLES. All right. How about a *"document"*?

OLD ANGUS. Well yes maybe a *document*...

CHARLES. Okay, well, *that document* –

OLD ANGUS. – was no fuckin' *contract*, let me tell you!

MACKENZIE STEWART. It was like one piece o' paper.

OLD ANGUS. And not even a full page at that.

ONE OF THE OTHERS. Mine was just a paragraph!

CHARLES. Right. Well clearly there's been a mix-up here.

OLD ANGUS. To say the least!

CHARLES. Right. Let me ask you something...

MACKENZIE STEWART. Actually, before you do, I think maybe we need to confer. Excuse us, would you?

*(**MACKENZIE STEWART** leads everyone into an adjoining room, everyone muttering as they go. **CHARLES** stares after them, shaken. Only he and **FELICITY** remain.)*

CHARLES. What do *you* make of this?

FELICITY. Not sure. But it doesn't look promising.

CHARLES. Certainly does not.

*(**CHARLES**'s briefcase starts to ring.)*

Oh God...

(**CHARLES** *opens his briefcase, revealing an elaborate, multi-part telecommunications system.*)

FELICITY. Is that a *phone?*

CHARLES. Phone uhhhh…*system.* Satellite.

(*It's a lot to set up. The phone keeps ringing.*)

FELICITY. …Don't they make them *smaller?*

CHARLES. Yes, absolutely. But not nearly as powerful. This one can reach…well, *anywhere*…assuming there's a clear patch of sky. *Mr. Bruce?* Just a tiny opening will do…

FELICITY. Well it is Scotland, after all.

CHARLES. I tried to tell him that. *Mr. Bruce?*

(*He waits a moment more, then hangs up, glumly puts the gear back into the case. Shuts the case. Stares out.*)

FELICITY. What happens if he can't reach you?

CHARLES. It's not good.

FELICITY. Well if it's any help, there's a payphone just outside. In fact I may even have some…Yes!

(*She starts pulling out fistfuls of coins.*)

CHARLES. You come prepared.

FELICITY. I try to be.

CHARLES. (*scooping up the coins*) And it's…

FELICITY. Just outside.

(**CHARLES** *walks out of the pub and into the rain and the night. She watches him go.*)

(*Then she notices the Green Man's rose on the floor, and picks it up. Stares at it.*)

(*The rumble of thunder is in the distance.*)

Scene 3

(Moments later, outside the pub, side of building, **CHARLES** *in a phone booth, on the phone. Note that a path runs past the booth and the pub, leading toward a distant hill.)*

(On another side of the stage, in a shaft of light, we see **ROBERT BRUCE,** *on his end of the line.)*

(Note that the double slashes represent points of interruption.)

CHARLES. Hello?

ROBERT BRUCE. Pearse! There you are, what the fuck, Alice had you on speed dial // for the last two hours.

CHARLES. Mr. Bruce, can you hear me?

ROBERT BRUCE. Pearse?

CHARLES. Mr. Bruce, it's CHARLES, can // you hear me?

ROBERT BRUCE. I know, fuck yes, I can hear you.

CHARLES. Wait, wait there's a delay, // a few second delay. So –

ROBERT BRUCE. I'm here. I can hear you.

CHARLES. Don't talk if you hear blank space, all right? *(pause)* Um, …Mr. Bruce? …*Hello?*

ROBERT BRUCE. I heard blank space so I bit my fucking tongue.

CHARLES. Oh, no, sorry sir, I was just letting you know about the // delay.

ROBERT BRUCE. So how's it going? Have we resumed construction yet?

CHARLES. Well I've only been here a few // hours now so it's still a bit early in the game.

ROBERT BRUCE. Because I want this thing moving forward.

CHARLES. Sir, wait for my answer, // all right?

ROBERT BRUCE. *Delay?* I'm not waiting a fucking second longer.

CHARLES. Yes, sir. There's this delay you see, in the phone line, and so –

ROBERT BRUCE. *What* delay? This is not the kind of news I was expecting.

CHARLES. No, sir. And // if you would just hear me out –

ROBERT BRUCE. I sent you there to get things *moving!*

CHARLES. Yes, sir. And I will. But first I // need to ascertain exactly –

ROBERT BRUCE. Because I want this on a *fast*-track!

CHARLES. Yes, sir. And it will be.

ROBERT BRUCE. I think something's wrong with this connection.

CHARLES. That could be. // It's just something that –

ROBERT BRUCE. And by the way, what have you done with all those fucking *corpses?*

CHARLES. Actually I'm still in the // process of analyzing –

ROBERT BRUCE. I hope you've gotten rid of them by now.

CHARLES. Well not exactly, no.

ROBERT BRUCE. Well then get rid of them.

CHARLES. Yes. Well. I think the idea of you donating a *wing* shows a lot of promise.

ROBERT BRUCE. What the fuck are you talking about?

CHARLES. To the British Museum. You know, to *house* them all. // Sir, we went over this.

ROBERT BRUCE. *House?*

CHARLES. Store, display, all those, you know, // *bodies.*

ROBERT BRUCE. Oh yes! "The Robert Bruce Collection of Shit Found in the Ground Wing." // I like that name.

CHARLES. Yes, well actually I told her you wouldn't even need to take credit. // So I'm not –

ROBERT BRUCE. Wouldn't *what?*

CHARLES. Take *credit.*

ROBERT BRUCE. I don't understand. // I can't hear you. *Pearse?*

CHARLES. Dammit. Sir, are you there? Because I seem to be running out of coins. Sir, I'm sorry, can // you hear me?

ROBERT BRUCE. *Coins?*

CHARLES. Yes sir, because // the satellite phone –

(As he talks, he locates a few more coins and deposits them.)

ROBERT BRUCE. Are you at a fucking *payphone?*

CHARLES. Yes, sir. The satellite doesn't work with all these // clouds.

ROBERT BRUCE. What?

CHARLES. Clouds! Too many // *clouds!*

ROBERT BRUCE. So then call me from your hotel! *Clouds?*

CHARLES. There *are* no hotels. // This is a very small –

ROBERT BRUCE. No *hotels?*

CHARLES. No, sir. // As I said, this is a very small –

ROBERT BRUCE. Well then we'll just have to *build* some, won't we?

CHARLES. Yes sir, but we can't build them // by *tomorrow.*

ROBERT BRUCE. 'Cause we need hotels.

CHARLES. Yes, sir, and we will get them, but // right now –

ROBERT BRUCE. So have we resumed construction yet?

CHARLES. Sir, I am about to run out of coins, and I don't want to cut you off.

(sound of the payphone, beeping)

ROBERT BRUCE. What's that sound?

CHARLES. The phone, asking for more coins, // which I do not have.

ROBERT BRUCE. Well then use your credit card!

CHARLES. It doesn't *take* credit cards! It's an old fashioned // payphone.

ROBERT BRUCE. What kind of hotel doesn't take credit cards?

CHARLES. Sir, how about I call you back when I // have more coins, and some actual news?

ROBERT BRUCE. Because I don't have patience for this. I have sunk twenty million into this goddam fucking golf course, so let's get it moving! You're supposed to *fix* things, not slow them down.

(As he talks, the eerie sound of a woman singing something in Gaelic is heard, which **CHARLES** *notices but* **ROBERT BRUCE** *of course does not.)*

*(***CHARLES** *looks toward the singing, startled)*

...do you hear me, Pearse? ...*Pearse?*

(An old **WASHERWOMAN** *now emerges from the path that leads past the pub. She is the one who's singing. She carries a washboard, and a man's distinctive shirt.)*

*(***CHARLES** *watches, incredulous, as she passes by, seemingly oblivious of both him and the rain, and heads up the hill.)*

Pearse! Are you there? ...Pearse, speak to me.

CHARLES. *(eyes still on the* **WASHERWOMAN***)* Sir, I'm afraid I'm out of coins now.

ROBERT BRUCE. *Pearse?*

CHARLES. If you can hear me, I'll call back when I know more.

(He hangs up and stares after the old woman.)

ROBERT BRUCE. Pearse? Something tells me you're holding out on me...*Pearse?*...

(Lights off on **ROBERT BRUCE.***)*

(Enter **MACKENZIE STEWART**, *from the front of the pub.)*

MACKENZIE STEWART. Ah, there y'are! Mr. Morgan has found Mr. Ross. They're waiting for ya upstairs in my office. I thought ya might be wantin' some privacy for this...*Mr. Pearse?*

CHARLES. What? ...Oh, yes. Good.

*(He leads **CHARLES** off, **CHARLES** still gazing off in the direction the **WASHERWOMAN** was heading, which is up the hill.)*

(Distant rumble of thunder is heard.)

Scene 4

(**MACKENZIE STEWART**'s *office on the second floor of the pub. The room has two doors, one leading to the main staircase and the pub below, the other to a back entrance.*)

(*It also contains a desk, coal-burning fireplace, unlit at the moment, an old couch with* **CHARLES**'s *luggage stacked nearby, and several chairs, one occupied by* **WILLIAM ROSS**, *60s, shivering badly despite the wool cap pulled down over his head, several scarves around his neck, and multiple layers of thick sweaters wrapped around his body.* **HARRY MORGAN** *stands nearby, briefcase in hand.*)

HARRY MORGAN. What if I get you some water?

ROSS. *(teeth chattering)* I hate this water. Like drinkin' fffffuckin' grrrravel.

HARRY MORGAN. What about aspirin?

ROSS. I took a ffffistful before we left. I shouldn't be out at all, ya know! I should be home under a ton o' blankets, like ya found me. Are you sure there's no window open? 'Cause I swear I can feel a ffffuckin' drrrraft.

HARRY MORGAN. *(mimicking* **ROSS***)* 'Cause you're in fffffuckin' Ssssscotland! Here, put this on.

(*He grabs a blanket from the couch and wraps it around* **ROSS**.)

ROSS. How about the rug?

HARRY MORGAN. On top of *this?*

ROSS. Why not? Snug as a bug!

HARRY MORGAN. I am not wrapping you in a goddam rug.

ROSS. The way I feel, it'll be my coffin next.

HARRY MORGAN. Fine, here, take my jacket.

ROSS. Thank you. You're a good man, Harry Morgan. Ya really are.

(**HARRY MORGAN** *puts his jacket around* **ROSS**.)

ROSS. *(cont.)* Despite what people say.

> (**HARRY MORGAN** *sighs. The back door opens and* **MACKENZIE STEWART** *enters with* **CHARLES.** *Wind blows in with them. Rain too.)*

This bloody climate'll be the death o' me yet.

HARRY MORGAN. Charles Pearse, William Ross. He was at home.

ROSS. Too sick to get out of bed, but I did for you. Pleased to make yer acquaintance, Mr. Pearse. Mackenzie, be a sweetheart and light the fffire, would ya?

MACKENZIE STEWART. Fire comin' up!

ROSS. This bloody climate'll be the death o' me yet.

MACKENZIE STEWART. *(to* **CHARLES,** *as he lights the fire)* By the way, this is where you'll be stayin'. As you can see, your luggage has been brought up. It's not the Ritz, I know…

CHARLES. It'll do fine.

> *(The fire is now lit.)*

MACKENZIE STEWART. There, that should help. I'll be just downstairs in the pub. Holler if ya need anythin'.

> *(Exit* **MACKENZIE STEWART.** *The moment he's gone,* **CHARLES** *turns and glares at* **ROSS.)***

ROSS. …Somethin' tells me you're wwwaitin' for me t' ssspeak.

CHARLES. Don't you think you should?

ROSS. Well, yes, given the circumstances. So let me begin by sayin' that if I have somehow been the cause of any awkwardness or confusion I do hereby apologize.

CHARLES. Why didn't you tell us about those bodies?

ROSS. Ah. That.

CHARLES. Yes, that. And don't tell me you didn't know, because you *had* to; you *live* here.

ROSS. Right, yes, *but –*

CHARLES. Not full-time, no, I understand. But certainly long enough to know what's what. Which is why you were made the POINT man on this goddam project!

HARRY MORGAN. Tell 'm!

ROSS. Right, yes, well, you see unfortunately I didn't realize there were so *many*.

CHARLES. How many bodies did you *think* there were?

ROSS. I don't know. One, maybe two.

CHARLES. Now to *me* – and perhaps this is just me – but to *me*, even *two* would seem too many. What do you think, Harry?

HARRY MORGAN. I agree.

CHARLES. So why didn't you tell us this?

ROSS. It didn't occur to me.

CHARLES. Didn't *occur* to you?

ROSS. These things are all *over* Scotland!

CHARLES. But surely not in numbers like this.

ROSS. No! And that's what I didn't realize. No one did! And if I'd so much as suspected there were so many, I would have told you instantly! But NO one knew! And if you don't believe me, I brought the engineers' report. It's in my bag. Where is the damn thing?

CHARLES. It's all right. I believe you.

HARRY MORGAN. So what do we do?

CHARLES. Well obviously we need to get rid of them.

ROSS. That museum woman! What about her?

HARRY MORGAN. Did she seem interested?

CHARLES. She did.

HARRY MORGAN. Well this is good.

CHARLES. Except the townsfolk want them all put back in the ground, which does not help our cause.

ROSS. I wouldn't take that too seriously.

CHARLES. Really.

ROSS. No, they're just sayin' that.

CHARLES. Why would they do that?

ROSS. To get a better deal. These people are not dummies. They know what's at stake.

CHARLES. Well now that's interesting. Because actually I'm not sure they do.

ROSS. ...well of course they do.

CHARLES. I don't think so. So why don't we find out? Be right back.

(exit **CHARLES**, *through the door that leads to the pub*)

(*awkward silence*)

(*finally...*)

ROSS. Actually, I think I could use a whiskey around now. Would you mind? I believe he keeps it in that cabinet there. But not that Drummhicit shite. *That's all I need...*

(**HARRY MORGAN** *goes to the cabinet.*)

HARRY MORGAN. Laphroaig?

ROSS. Too peaty.

HARRY MORGAN. Glenkinchie?

ROSS. Too grassy.

HARRY MORGAN. Well that's it then...except for a bottle of rum.

ROSS. What kind?

HARRY MORGAN. Can't read the name but there's a picture of a pirate on the label.

ROSS. Sounds like just the ticket.

HARRY MORGAN. One glass of rum comin' up.

(**CHARLES** *re-enters with* **MACKENZIE STEWART**.)

MACKENZIE STEWART. Gentlemen!

ROSS. Forget the rum.

CHARLES. So. Mackenzie, earlier today, I was talking to all of you about our *plans*...

MACKENZIE STEWART. Oh yes...

CHARLES. And I mentioned a *bridge*.

MACKENZIE STEWART. So you did.

CHARLES. And none of you seemed to know what the hell I was referring to.

MACKENZIE STEWART. That is correct.

CHARLES. Thank you. I only ask because suddenly I wondered if maybe I'd misunderstood.

MACKENZIE STEWART. No-no, Mr. Ross never mentioned anything to us about no bridge.

HARRY MORGAN. *Jesus Christ.*

CHARLES. But surely in your *contracts...*

MACKENZIE STEWART. *What* contracts?

HARRY MORGAN. I don't fuckin' believe this.

(**ROSS** *slides down deeper into his multi-layered clothing.*)

CHARLES. But certainly you all must've signed *something.* I mean, this is your land.

MACKENZIE STEWART. Yes, but not what I would call a *contract.* No, what I was trying to explain is that what I signed, and I believed the others signed, was more like what I would call a *receipt.*

CHARLES. A receipt...

MACKENZIE STEWART. Yes. In exchange for which Mr. Ross gave us all some money. Mine was in a paper bag.

CHARLES. Do you remember how much that payment was?

MACKENZIE STEWART. Oh yes indeed, because it was extremely generous... *(to* **ROSS***)* Is it all right if I say?

(**ROSS** *is now so hidden one can hardly see his face.*)

HARRY MORGAN. I believe he just nodded.

MACKENZIE STEWART. It was three hundred pounds.

CHARLES. *That much!*

MACKENZIE STEWART. I know. Needless to say, we were all very happy.

CHARLES. And for this, you gave up title to your land.

MACKENZIE STEWART. Oh no! We could not do that. That's not possible. No, this simply gave Mr. Ross and his group permission to explore.

CHARLES. *"Explore"*…

MACKENZIE STEWART. The land. You know, for the proposed golf course. Bear in mind though, most of that course will be on Mr. Ross's property, so maybe he signed a contract. You'd have to ask him about all that.

ROSS. *(to* **HARRY MORGAN,** *barely audible)* Could I maybe have that glass of rum?

HARRY MORGAN. Sorry, Willy. We're going to need you sober for this.

CHARLES. And what about the second course?

MACKENZIE STEWART. What second course?

CHARLES. Our plan calls for two golf courses, not just one.

MACKENZIE STEWART. …*two?*

CHARLES. Yes. With the first being relatively straightforward, and the other modeled more along the lines of St. Andrews, in hopes of attracting the British Open.

MACKENZIE STEWART. Oh my God…

CHARLES. On second thought, maybe you'd better give him that drink.

(**HARRY MORGAN** *goes to get* **ROSS** *a glass of rum)*

MACKENZIE STEWART. Make me one as well, if ya don't mind.

CHARLES. So you didn't know about this second course?

MACKENZIE STEWART. Not an inklin'. Forgive me, but where the hell would it go? 'Cause Mr. Ross's property can only hold one, and that's with a bit of a spill-over, which is why *we* got paid.

CHARLES. Well *currently,* the plan is for it to go out to the end of the promontory and sort of wrap around from there.

MACKENZIE STEWART. So…in other words…up the hill.

CHARLES. Yes…in fact, that's where the second course will end. The eighteenth green, I mean.

MACKENZIE STEWART. …on the *hill.*

CHARLES. Yes.

MACKENZIE STEWART. Just to be sure…are we talkin' 'bout the same hill?

CHARLES. It's the one you can sort of see from just outside the pub. You know, …at the end of the path… *That* one.

MACKENZIE STEWART. Right…well! …you see now, that is not possible. And, frankly, I am surprised to hear that you were even *considering* this 'cause Mr. Ross *knows* it's not possible.

(**ROSS** *is now trembling and shaking.*)

HARRY MORGAN. Why is that not possible?

MACKENZIE STEWART. Well because that's where the faeries live.

(long stunned silence)

HARRY MORGAN. *(finally)* No, he never told us that. We'd have remembered that.

MACKENZIE STEWART. Yes, well, anyway that's where they live. Or, to be more specific, underneath the *rock.*

CHARLES. What rock?

MACKENZIE STEWART. The one that's on top of the hill. Can't miss it! You should go up there. Though actually on second thought, maybe it's wiser if ya don't. But it's there, take my word, and under that rock is where they live.

HARRY MORGAN. What if we move the rock?

MACKENZIE STEWART. *Oh my God!*

HARRY MORGAN. Just a *little?*

MACKENZIE STEWART. NO! You cannot *touch* the thing!

CHARLES. *(to* **HARRY MORGAN***)* Let me handle this. *(to* **MACKENZIE STEWART***)* You say Mr. Ross knew about all this.

MACKENZIE STEWART. Oh yes. Everyone who lives here does.

CHARLES. *(to* **ROSS***)* I think maybe you should have told us this.

ROSS. Maybe I should have.

CHARLES. *(to* **MACKENZIE STEWART***)* You see we have a real problem now. Because, till this moment, Mr. Morgan and I – *and Mr. Bruce!* – have been operating under the belief that the Bog People were our main concern.

MACKENZIE STEWART. Oh no. Fuck the Bog People! Stick 'em back in the ground and you can play golf to your hearts' content. Which is not to say they won't keep poppin' up on ya, 'cause they will. I just mean that as a *group*, they don't care *what* ya do. Not so with the faeries.

CHARLES. They don't like people playing overhead.

MACKENZIE STEWART. No they do not. Mind you now, we have played up there. All of us have. Even Mr. Ross.But just a rag-tag kind of game, where you stick a pole in the ground and try to see who gets closest. But then, we know how to *deal* with the faeries, and therefore know when it's safe to play… Which is frankly not all that often.

CHARLES. When *is* it safe to play, if I may ask? As I'm sure Mr. Bruce will want to know. *(to* **HARRY MORGAN***)* Don't you think?

HARRY MORGAN. I would think.

MACKENZIE STEWART. Well off-hand I couldn't tell you definitively. It depends mostly on the month, but especially the moon. Still, I suppose we could probably work out some kind o' schedule.

CHARLES. That might be helpful.

MACKENZIE STEWART. Or maybe not. Faerie schedules are notoriously unreliable. No, I think your best bet is to stick to one course only. Which would seem to solve everything.

CHARLES. Unfortunately, it doesn't. Because of the *houses* we're planning to construct.

MACKENZIE STEWART. What houses?

HARRY MORGAN. The ones that will be lining the side of the second course.

MACKENZIE STEWART. Where the *faeries* live!

CHARLES. I thought they were only under the rock.

MACKENZIE STEWART. Oh, no-no, that's just their main *domicile.* No, they move around. You know. Like *us.*

CHARLES. So what do you propose we do? Besides just giving up.

MACKENZIE STEWART. Oh no, you don't wanna do that! No, this is way too important to us *all.* One way or another, we have got to work this out.

CHARLES. So what do you suggest?

MACKENZIE STEWART. Well I suppose you could try to negotiate.

CHARLES. …with the faeries?

MACKENZIE STEWART. Yes.

CHARLES. …have they got like a *lawyer?*

MACKENZIE STEWART. I don't know.

HARRY MORGAN. Probably too tiny to see.

MACKENZIE STEWART. Well that could be. But as a rule we don't negotiate with the faeries, so I can't say about the lawyer part for sure. In fact, now that I think of it, I've never even seen a *faerie.*

CHARLES. Ah-hah.

MACKENZIE STEWART. Indeed, come to think of it, I don't know anyone who has.

CHARLES. So how do you know they're there?

MACKENZIE STEWART. Well we see their *effect…* They look *out* for us. I mean, how does one know God is there? You see His effect. It's like that. *Except…*well, with the faeries it's more immediate. I mean, piss off a faerie and you'll know it right away. Which is not true with God. Or at least not in *my* experience. But that may just be me.

CHARLES. Right…*Harry?*

HARRY MORGAN. I'm…uhhhh, thinking.

CHARLES. Right. So! Let's say we wanted to negotiate.

MACKENZIE STEWART. I think that's the way to go.

CHARLES. Good. So how would we go about this? I mean, do we write a note? "Have your people call mine?" I'm not being funny, we need to know.

MACKENZIE STEWART. No, I understand. And as I said, I'm not sure.

CHARLES. Well who is? Because *someone* obviously communicates with them, since you all seem to know the fucking rules!

MACKENZIE STEWART. *Maybe the fisherman!*

CHARLES. The "fisherman."

MACKENZIE STEWART. Yes. He was in the pub. Old guy. You may have met him. His daughter, Fiona, the saucy one with the fiery red hair, she helps out, I'm pretty sure you met her.

CHARLES. Oh yes!

MACKENZIE STEWART. I think *they* might know.

CHARLES. Why?

MACKENZIE STEWART. Well it's just a rumor really, but some folks think they *speak* to them. But that's not certain. Still, if anybody does, it's most likely them. But then again, maybe not. I'm sorry; not sure I've been very helpful here.

CHARLES. No, you have. Indeed, I hate to think what might've happened if you hadn't told us this.

MACKENZIE STEWART. Don't know why Mr. Ross didn't tell you this *himself…*

CHARLES. No, but we'll find out soon enough.

MACKENZIE STEWART. So! If there's nothin' else, I'll go back downstairs. Holler if ya need.

(*Exit* MACKENZIE STEWART. *The moment he's gone…*)

CHARLES. It's a fucking scam!

ROSS. *Exactly!*

> (**CHARLES** *and* **HARRY MORGAN** *turn and glare at* **ROSS**.)

…oh no. I didn't mean myself.

HARRY MORGAN. Didn't you?

ROSS. No, I meant *them.* The townsfolk. They're gonna milk ya on this. *Faeries, indeed!*

CHARLES. So you don't believe all that.

ROSS. Please! What do ya take me for? Only fools believe shite like that. No, the question is, do *they* believe it? And frankly there I'm not sure. But they certainly believe it enough t' make things hot for all of you. Which is why I didn't tell you about all this.

CHARLES. I'm not sure I follow the logic of that.

ROSS. Well if I'd told you, you'd have had to tell Mr. Bruce, and we'd have been dead right off the bat.

HARRY MORGAN. We're dead now!

CHARLES. *I need a drink…*

> (**HARRY MORGAN** *joins* **CHARLES** *at the liquor cabinet.*)

HARRY MORGAN. What are you going to tell Robert?

CHARLES. Well obviously not this. Can *you* think of how to tell him this?

HARRY MORGAN. Not a clue.

ROSS. Which is why I didn't tell *you!*

HARRY MORGAN. Would you kindly do us all a favor and shut the hell up? *(to* **CHARLES**, *sotto voce) Maybe we should pull out.*

CHARLES. *What!?*

HARRY MORGAN. I am only saying —

CHARLES. Harry. Listen to me carefully, and repeat exactly what I say: "We are not pulling out."

HARRY MORGAN. "We are not pulling out."

CHARLES. And what do you suppose that means?

HARRY MORGAN. We are not pulling out?

CHARLES. And why do you think that is?

HARRY MORGAN. Because pulling out is not what you came here to do.

(**CHARLES** *makes a gesture: voila.*)

But! For just one moment –

CHARLES. *Harry?*

HARRY MORGAN. I will not bring it up again.

CHARLES. Thank you.

ROSS. What about me?

CHARLES. What *about* you?

ROSS. Can I bring it up again?

CHARLES. NO! *NO* ONE BRINGS IT UP! IT'S OFF THE FUCKING TABLE! One way or another, we are going to make this thing happen. Is that understood?

HARRY MORGAN. Understood.

CHARLES. Especially as there is about twenty million dollars of Mr. Bruce's money somewhere, lying around... *(turning to* **ROSS***)* Under your mattress, I would imagine.

ROSS. Oh no-no, much safer place than that.

CHARLES. *Cookie* jar?

ROSS. One can't put twenty million in a cookie jar. No, it's in a very safe place. Can't quite remember where off-hand. Maybe Harry has it. Harry, have you got the twenty mill?

HARRY MORGAN. Jesus Christ!

ROSS. I'm sorry, is anyone else hot in here but me?

CHARLES. No, just you.

ROSS. Suddenly I'm like, I don't know, burning up.

HARRY MORGAN. THEN TAKE SOMETHING OFF!

ROSS. Good idea.

(**ROSS** *starts to peel off his various layers.*)

(*As he does,* **HARRY MORGAN** *pours himself another drink and* **CHARLES** *downs his.*)

(**ROSS** *has soon stripped down to his regular shirt – a shirt we should all recognize if we've been paying proper attention.* **CHARLES** *spots the shirt.*)

CHARLES. That's the shirt I saw!

ROSS. What are you talking about?

CHARLES. That shirt…the one you have on…

ROSS. What about it?

CHARLES. Well…just before I came in here, I was outside on the phone with Mr. Bruce, and…well, it was so strange, but suddenly I heard this eerie *singing*…and the next thing I know, an old woman comes walking down that path – the one that leads up to the hill Mackenzie was –

…well that one. And she was holding this washboard, and what looked just like…well, that shirt there. The one he has on.

ROSS. Oh my God, oh my God… *(etc.)*

(the following dialogue should overlap)

CHARLES. But it can't be yours, because there you are with it on. // And this happened a short while ago.

ROSS. No, it's mine, oh God, oh my God, // get me home, Harry, quick, you've gotta get me home. *(etc.)*

HARRY MORGAN. Willie, stop, sit down, Willie, Willie, // for God sakes, stop this, Willie, Willie… *(etc.)*

ROSS. Oh God, oh my God, I'm gonna die, I don't wanna die, I'm gonna die, oh my God… *(etc.)*

(**CHARLES** *rushes out and down the hall, shouting as he goes…*)

CHARLES. *(offstage)* MACKENZIE! COME QUICKLY! MACKENZIE! *MACKENZIE! (etc.)*

ROSS. *(continuing uninterrupted)* Harry get me home, I'm gonna die, I don't wanna die, I'm gonna die, oh my God, Harry get me home, I'm gonna die, Harry please get me home, oh my God… *(etc.)*

(Now we hear **CHARLES** *and* **MACKENZIE STEWART** *racing to the room.)*

MACKENZIE STEWART. *(offstage)* What is it? What's happened?

CHARLES. *(offstage)* I don't know. Something weird! Not sure!

(The two men rush in. The moment **ROSS** *sees* **MACKENZIE STEWART**…*)*

ROSS. He saw the washerwoman!

MACKENZIE STEWART. *Who* did?

ROSS. *He* did! Outside. And she had my shirt!

MACKENZIE STEWART. Your *shirt?*

ROSS. This very one!

MACKENZIE STEWART. *(to* **CHARLES**, *incredulous)* She had this shirt?

CHARLES. Yes.

ROSS. And he saw it, she had it, and // she was going up the hill to wash it! And she was singin'! Oh my God, oh my God… *(etc.)*

HARRY MORGAN. Willy, Willy, it's all right, calm down *(etc.)*

MACKENZIE STEWART. *(simultaneously)* All right, lift him up, help him up, we've got to get him home, come on now, help him up, that's it, help him up, here we go, that's it, here we go…

ROSS. *(overlapping)* He saw her, he did, outside, with *my shirt!* Oh my God, oh my God…

*(***HARRY MORGAN*** grabs* **ROSS** *under one arm,* **MACKENZIE STEWART** *the other, and together they walk him toward the door. As they go…)*

I don't wanna die, I'm gonna die, I don't wanna die… *(etc.)*

MACKENZIE STEWART. Stop that now, you're not gonna die.

ROSS. No, I am, and I know why, I do, and I deserve it! I do! *(to* **HARRY MORGAN**) AND YOU ARE THE REASON,

HARRY MORGAN! YOU ARE! AND YOU KNOW IT! AND SHE'S GONNA WASH *YOUR SHIRT NEXT!*

CHARLES. What's he talking about?

HARRY MORGAN. I don't know.

ROSS. Yes you do! And I'm gonna die because of it! Oh God, oh my God…

(*to* **MACKENZIE STEWART,** *as* **CHARLES** *and* **HARRY MORGAN** *lead* **ROSS** *from the room:*)

CHARLES. What is this?

MACKENZIE STEWART. (*as they go*) It's nothin'…nothin'… nothin' at all.

(*They exit,* **ROSS** *crying out as they go…*)

ROSS. I don't wanna die, Harry, help me, I don't wanna die, I really don't (*etc.*)

(**CHARLES** *watches them leave, stunned*)

(*then…*)

(*He stares out, shaken.*)

(*And then suddenly he feels the heat, and loosens his collar and tie. It's still too hot. So he goes to the window and opens it. Blessed air! He breathes it in deeply. Which is when he hears, from somewhere outside…*)

FELICITY. (*offstage*) Mr. Pearse? …Mr. Pearse?

(*He looks out. But it's still raining out and difficult to see.*)

…Over here! It's Felicity! I need to speak to you! It's important! Can you come down?

(**CHARLES** *heads for the back door, spots the bottle he's been using, pours one more drink, downs it, and then rushes out.*)

(*The sound of rain continues, rumble of thunder in the distance.*)

Scene 5

(Moments later, outside the pub, a flash of lightning reveals **FELICITY**, *in raingear and heavy-duty backpack, standing under a sheltering tree near the phonebooth, and the path the* **WASHERWOMAN** *took, a distinctive scarf wrapped around her neck.)*

(Now another flash reveals **CHARLES** *emerging from the rear of the building, jacket pulled over his head against the rain.)*

(FELICITY *has a flashlight. She shines it.)*

FELICITY. *Mr. Pearse! (As he hurries over, she pulls a poncho from a pocket.)* Here, take this. I always carry extras. What the hell was happening up there?

CHARLES. What do you mean?

FELICITY. I was in the pub waiting for you when Mr. Mackenzie and Mr. Morgan practically carry this old drunk down the stairs and out the door, with everyone running after them, half of them in hysterics, the other half muttering something about a washerwoman.

CHARLES. I'm not sure what it's about.

FELICITY. Well that's fair enough. It's a strange place all right. I'm sure you've noticed by now.

CHARLES. I have indeed.

(rain really coming down)

Listen, could we not do this inside?

FELICITY. No. This needs to be private. Mr. Pearse, what I wanted to tell you was that I wasn't completely honest with you before, when you made that generous offer about the wing. The fact is, I can't accept. The museum doesn't want those bodies. And I knew it when I came.

CHARLES. Why?

FELICITY. They think they're commonplace. Bog People are all over Europe. The Dublin Museum displays theirs prominently. "Do you want tourists to think we're competing with Ireland?"

CHARLES. Then why come here at all?

FELICITY. Things aren't always what they seem, Mr. Pearse. I'm onto something here, I know it, and some o' these people do, too. And the ones who do don't want me sniffing around, which only makes my nose more curious. *What are they hiding?* Well I now think that puzzle lies at the heart of this. And if I can solve it, the museum *will* take these bodies.

CHARLES. What do you need to do?

FELICITY. A little more digging, when no one's watching. *And I could use your help.*

CHARLES. …in what way?

FELICITY. We need to see what lies under the rock at the top of this hill. Here, one for you, one for me.

(*She unhooks two shovels from her backpack and holds out one for him.*)

CHARLES. I'm sorry, but…why the rock?

FELICITY. Because it's the one place they've told me not to dig… So. Shall we go?

(*pause*)

CHARLES. …Okay. I'm not saying your plan's no good. But surely one needs more reasons than just that. I mean, look at this weather!

FELICITY. Exactly! Who goes out in weather like this? Which is why no one will see us. If they discover what we're doing, I'll be out of here, and there goes your plan as well.

CHARLES. Yes, but…

FELICITY. Something's scaring you.

CHARLES. NOTHING'S scaring me! This is just not the sort of thing I do.

FELICITY. Well then maybe it's about time you did.

CHARLES. Fine, and I will take that into account, just not tonight.

FELICITY. You have other plans?

CHARLES. Yes, actually. Something has come up which I need to talk to Mr. Morgan about. Sorry.

(He starts to leave.)

FELICITY. You're making a big mistake, Mr. Pearse.
(That stops him.)

(He looks back at her.)

Opportunities like this don't come along very often. Surely Mr. Morgan can wait.
(She fixes him with an intense gaze.)

(when he does not move…)

Hold this, would you?
(She hands him her shovel.)

What is this?
(She pulls a noose from one of her pockets.)

CHARLES. A noose.

FELICITY. And if I do this with it?
(She slips it around her head, long end dangling down.)

CHARLES. A noose…that's not doing its job.

FELICITY. And what if I now attach a flower right here…
(She extracts a rose from another pocket and slips its stem through the knot.)

…the way the Green Man was wearing his. Or didn't you notice that?

CHARLES. I didn't.

FELICITY. Well I did. *Instantly.* What is it now, Mr. Pearse?

CHARLES. It's…

FELICITY. No longer a noose, but an *amulet.*

CHARLES. …an *amulet?*

FELICITY. From the Latin *amuletum*, meaning "an object that protects a person from harm."

CHARLES. How does a noose protect you from harm?

FELICITY. What does a noose remind you of?

CHARLES. Death.

FELICITY. What else?

CHARLES. I give up.

FELICITY. "Fertility."

CHARLES. A *noose?*

FELICITY. Did you not notice the Green Man's phallus?

CHARLES. Yes, but how was that connected to his noose?

(She thinks a moment. Then…)

FELICITY. Have you ever tried to strangle yourself while having sex?

CHARLES. …I have not.

FELICITY. Well I have done it to a few men, and the effect on the penis is remarkable, and immediate.

CHARLES. Is it?

FELICITY. It really is. *If you see what I'm getting at.*

CHARLES. …you think the Bog People were going down there to get *laid?*

FELICITY. *Transcendentally.*

(pause)

CHARLES. I'm not sure I'm following this.

FELICITY. Oh, I think you are. You're just not used to opening your mind in this particular way…take a good look at the Bog People's faces next time you can. Those men were not dead when they descended, nor were they afraid. They were *excited.*

CHARLES. Where did they think they were going?

FELICITY. Ah, where indeed. If only we knew that…

CHARLES. Where do *you* think they were going?

FELICITY. Oh, I think they were going to their deaths. No, your first question is the right one. Where did they *think* they were going? ...and why were they all looking in the same direction?

(*He stares at her. What?*)

If you draw a line from where their eyes were all aiming, those lines meet in one place.

CHARLES. *The rock.*

FELICITY. You got it. No, Mr. Pearse, something far more erotic than peat suffuses the soil of this fair land. And unless I miss my guess, the hot spot is that rock. So, wha'd'ya say? The Bog People took a leap into the Unknown. Why don't we?

(*pause*)

CHARLES. Right. Well! As I was saying earlier, I really need to meet with Mr. Morgan, and –

FELICITY. Why are you trembling?

CHARLES. I'm not trembling, this is *shivering!* It's raining, it's fucking freezing out here! Look, tell you what, wait till tomorrow, I'll get my construction crew –

FELICITY. NO! For an enterprise like this, rain is our ally.

CHARLES. Yes, but this is a bit more than just rain.

FELICITY. *Exactly!* Which is why we need to go *now!*

(*A loud crash of thunder is heard.*)

Hear that? That is no ordinary thunder, Mr. Pearse. That is the hill, warning us to stay away. Why? What is it hiding? And what would that rock tell us if it could speak?

(*Suddenly, the phone rings, startling them both.*)

CHARLES. Maybe that's the museum!

FELICITY. I don't think so.

(*It keeps ringing.*)

CHARLES. ...well shouldn't we at least answer it?

(**FELICITY**, *fed up with this delay, answers it*)

FELICITY. Hello?

ROBERT BRUCE. *(offstage) Where the fuck is Pearse?*

FELICITY. It's for you.

ROBERT BRUCE. *(offstage)* PEARSE!? …I know you're there, Pearse. I can feel you breathing!

CHARLES. I should probably take this.

FELICITY. Right.

ROBERT BRUCE. *(offstage) PEARSE!*

FELICITY. Fine. I'll do it myself!

(She hands him the phone, and stalks off toward the hill.)

ROBERT BRUCE. *(offstage)* Speak to me, Pearse! …Pearse?

*(**CHARLES** stares at the phone, not sure whether he actually wants to take this call…)*

*(When suddenly the **WASHERWOMAN** reappears, same place as before, same paraphernalia in her hands – but a different shirt. Due to the light, we can't quite make it out.)*

*(She passes near **CHARLES**. He stares at her.)*

…Pearse?

*(As if sensing him, the **WASHERWOMAN** stops and looks him in the eye. A flash of lightning reveals…*

(FELICITY'S SCARF IN HER HANDS!)

*(The **WASHERWOMAN** smiles at **CHARLES**.)*

(And then she continues on, same direction as **FELICITY**.*)*

CHARLES. *Oh my God…*

(It takes him a moment more to decide what to do. And then he does it: lets the phone just dangle there, and rushes off in the same direction, route illumined by the lightning.)

Felicity!

(A tremendous thunder clap is heard. And then the lightning fades, and **CHARLES** *disappears from view, and everything grows dark.)*

(In the dark, we can make out **ROBERT BRUCE** *shouting* **CHARLES***'s name.)*

End of Act One

ACT 2

(The Fisherman's Hut.)

(Night. **FIONA,** *cowering in a corner. Raging wind, thunder, lightning, pouring rain.)*

(But there's something else going on here, too; an eerie kind of sound, could easily be part of the wind, or maybe not.)

(Then, from somewhere in the distance…)

OLD ANGUS. *(offstage)* Fiona!

(But she does not hear, her focus being elsewhere)

Fiona!

(She still does not hear.)

FIONA, FOR GOD SAKES, HELP ME!

(Now she hears and races to the door. Flings it open. Rain pours in. Ferocious wind.)

FIONA. Dad?

OLD ANGUS. *(offstage)* Over here! I can't hold 'm anymore! *Hurry!*

(She runs off.)

(a moment later…)

FIONA. *(offstage)* Oh my God!

OLD ANGUS. *(offstage)* Here, grab his legs. Easy now.

FIONA. *(offstage)* Is he alive?

OLD ANGUS. *(offstage)* I dunno. He was before, but just barely.

(Enter, **FIONA** *and* **OLD ANGUS** *carrying* **CHARLES,** *no signs of life, the poncho* **FELICITY** *gave him in tatters, his metal briefcase charred almost beyond recognition.)*

(**OLD ANGUS**, *in a slicker, kicks the door shut.*)

OLD ANGUS. Lay 'm over here…

(*They lay him on a couch.*)

FIONA. What happened?

OLD ANGUS. He went up the hill.

FIONA. Oh my God!

OLD ANGUS. Better get some blankets. He's near frozen.

(*She runs for blankets.*)

Good, there's still a pulse. And get some whiskey, too!

(*She runs back with blankets and whiskey.*)

We'll have to get him out o' these.

FIONA. I'll get 'm a robe!

(*Now she races out of the room.*)

OLD ANGUS. AND RUN A BATH WHILE YOU'RE AT IT!

FIONA. *(offstage)* I'M ON THE CASE!

CHARLES. *Where am I?*

OLD ANGUS. In my hut, safe and sound.

CHARLES. And who, pray, are you?

OLD ANGUS. The fisherman. And that's me daughter comin' in with the robe. Ya met us in the pub.

CHARLES. What pub?

OLD ANGUS. The one you were in before you went up that hill. Here, drink this.

CHARLES. No-no. *Anything but that!*

OLD ANGUS. It's all right, this stuff's drinkable.

CHARLES. You're right. That's not bad.

OLD ANGUS. Now what were you doin' on that hill?

CHARLES. I can't remember.

OLD ANGUS. Maybe this'll refresh your memory.

(*He holds up **CHARLES**' charred briefcase.*)

CHARLES. *Oh my God!*

OLD ANGUS. That's right, oh my God. You're a lucky man, Mr. Pearse. How that bolt o' lightning didn't strike you along with this we'll never know. Get my cutter. Might as well clip it off entirely.

(**FIONA** *runs for his wire-cutter.*)

CHARLES. *I thought I was going to die…*

OLD ANGUS. Because you *were*. And you can thank my daughter that you didn't.

FIONA. What do you mean?

OLD ANGUS. You told me you felt there was somethin' wrong.

FIONA. Yes, but I didn't know what.

OLD ANGUS. No, but you had that look. And I know enough by now not to disregard those looks, so out I went. And if I hadn't, he'd be cinders himself, if not worse.

(*Using the wire-cutter, he cuts the chain.*)

There. Free at last.

CHARLES. FELICITY!

OLD ANGUS. What about her?

CHARLES. She's still up there! I was following her, but she didn't see me. Then all hell broke loose and I lost sight of her. *You've got to go get her!*

OLD ANGUS. She's already down.

CHARLES. What do you mean?

OLD ANGUS. I mean she ran down on her own, screamin' like a banshee. That's how I spotted you, silhouetted up there against the lightnin', wavin' your arms like a dyin' bird, and screamin' like a banshee yerself. What happened up there, Mr. Pearse? Tell my daughter. Though I did see it myself, I still cannot quite believe it.

CHARLES. The ground started to open up.

OLD ANGUS. Scared shitless, weren't ya?

CHARLES. *Oh my God…*

OLD ANGUS. The rock is what saved 'm. He'd climbed on top of it.

FIONA. And it *let* him?

OLD ANGUS. So it seems. *What were you doin' on that hill, Mr. Pearse?*

CHARLES. I wanted to see what it was like.

OLD ANGUS. Why?

CHARLES. We're planning to put part of our golf course up there.

OLD ANGUS. Well then you're out o' your fuckin' minds.

FIONA. *Glinna ei d^ol l^u.**

OLD ANGUS. I agree.

FIONA. *Doorst brukanni?*

OLD ANGUS. *Brukanni! Doorst brukanni!*

FIONA. *Basvittu! Cara d^orta!*

OLD ANGUS. *(unless…) Unglayna…*

FIONA. Unglayna…

CHARLES. I'm sorry. Is that Gaelic?

OLD ANGUS. No.

FIONA. Sit up.

CHARLES. *What?*

OLD ANGUS. Sit up and lean forward.

FIONA. We need to check something.

(**CHARLES** *does as they bid and leans forward.* **FIONA** *pulls out his shirt and peers down his back.*)

Look at this.

(**OLD ANGUS** *looks.*)

OLD ANGUS. How long have you had this?

---

*Because the audience will be not be able to understand what Angus and Fiona are saying any more than Charles, the reader should not either. But the actors will know what they're saying, so the *intention* behind their words will be clear. For the reader who's not satisfied with this, a version of this exchange, *with translation*, has been appended at the back. However, it should not be looked at now or the effect of this scene will be undermined. If you must, look at it later.

CHARLES. What?

FIONA. This stain.

CHARLES. What stain?

OLD ANGUS. On your left shoulder blade.

CHARLES. I don't know what you're talking about.

OLD ANGUS. Get him a mirror.

> (**FIONA** *runs, gets a mirror, runs back and holds it up behind* **CHARLES**' *shoulder.*)

CHARLES. I've never seen it before.

FIONA. *Gleena deesfu-deegy.*

OLD ANGUS. *Su, githwynith y vaethor boe ben y d^barametta.*

FIONA. *Y á tirë.*

> (**FIONA** *gets a box of salt, and starts sprinkling salt around.*)

CHARLES. Excuse me, but what is your daughter doing?

OLD ANGUS. Sprinkling salt around the room. *Nungin du-fenneltassa!*

FIONA. Right.

> (*She hurries to the window and spreads salt along the sill.*)

OLD ANGUS. *Un duportlenacka!*

FIONA. I know, I know.

> (*Finished with the window, she spreads salt by the door jam. As she works …*)
>
> *Marku d^ulma una peetafeern?*

OLD ANGUS. Good idea.

> (*While* **FIONA** *completes her tasks,* **OLD ANGUS** *starts a peat fire.*)

CHARLES. Though a little more heat would definitely be welcome, frankly I'm not so sure about that smell.

OLD ANGUS. That smell is what's important. *(to* **FIONA***)* What next?

FIONA. *P^inji, hithu gwann ma th^unga banya.*

OLD ANGUS. *Ahhh! Yo. Welsa! Modo-welsa! (to* **CHARLES***)* We have decided the time has come for you to take a bath.

CHARLES. ...really!

FIONA. So if you don't mind, would you please take your clothes off?

CHARLES. ...ummm, here?

OLD ANGUS. Here, or where the bath is, it doesn't really matter.

FIONA. Here's your robe.

CHARLES. ...right.

(*She holds out the robe.*)

Why do I get the feeling something is going on here that I don't understand?

OLD ANGUS. Because something *is* going on that you don't understand.

FIONA. But if it makes you feel any better, we don't fully understand it either.

OLD ANGUS. But we at least understand it more than you.

FIONA. *Take the robe.*

CHARLES. ...by any chance, is this some kind of magic robe?

OLD ANGUS. Not that we know.

CHARLES. Right. (*He takes the robe.*) And the bathtub is in *there?*

OLD ANGUS. Right in there.

CHARLES. And I can undress in there?

OLD ANGUS. Or out here.

CHARLES. I think, if it's all right, I'll undress in there.

FIONA. Then I will too.

CHARLES. ...so...you'll be undressing as *well.*

OLD ANGUS. Well she'll be bathing *with* you.

CHARLES. Ah-hah.

OLD ANGUS. Is that all right?

CHARLES. Oh. Uhhh, yes! I mean...is the tub big enough?

FIONA. I would think.

CHARLES. Well then I guess that part at least is fine. I have to say, this is a very odd island.

OLD ANGUS. Doesn't seem so to us.

CHARLES. No, well you live here.

FIONA. Maybe you will too.

CHARLES. Yes, maybe. Or maybe not, who can say? I mean the ground almost swallowed me before, now I'm about to get into a bathtub with you, and Mr. Bruce is unaware of all of this.

FIONA. So, shall we go?

CHARLES. Why not? I mean what have I got to lose?

FIONA. I don't know.

CHARLES. Well then why don't we find out? *(to* **OLD ANGUS***)* Will you be out here, or are you coming too?

OLD ANGUS. The tub's not big enough for three.

CHARLES. Well then I guess you're out here.

FIONA. See you later, dad!

OLD ANGUS. Till later, dear!

> *(***CHARLES** *and* **FIONA** *exit into the room with the tub.)*

> *(***OLD ANGUS** *stares out.)*

> *(The wind howls.)*

> *(Gradually, the wind takes on an eerie kind of whistle, similar to the sound we heard at the start, when* **FIONA** *was alone; the sort that can make one's hair stand on end.)*

> *(***OLD ANGUS** *writes a note for* **FIONA**, *leaves it on the table, and starts to leave when the wind suddenly howls even more. So he decides to spread a little more salt around, just in case.* Then *he leaves.)*

> *(The lights fade.)*

> *(When the lights return, it's later that night.)*

(CHARLES and FIONA emerge from the bathroom in robes.)

FIONA. So I take it you enjoyed the bath.

CHARLES. Enjoyed is not the word. Loved, relished, was driven mad by, as well as scrubbed clean by…by the way, where's your father?

FIONA. *(having read OLD ANGUS's note)* He went into the village to let them know you're safe; no need for a search party.

CHARLES. None at all. HERE I AM!

FIONA. Would you like something to eat?

CHARLES. *Love* something to eat.

FIONA. How's smoked salmon sound?

CHARLES. Are you kidding?

FIONA. Yes, because we don't have it.

CHARLES. That's right. "No fish today!"

FIONA. Well, not lately.

CHARLES. So what is there to eat?

FIONA. Eggs?

CHARLES. Sounds good.

FIONA. So what do you do when you're not here?

CHARLES. Can we not talk about something more pleasant?

FIONA. Is what you do unpleasant?

CHARLES. Compared to your body, everything's unpleasant.

FIONA. Unfortunately, hard as this may be to believe, there is more to this world than my body.

CHARLES. You're right; I don't believe it.

FIONA. Well it's true.

CHARLES. Not for me. Not anymore.

FIONA. Okay, then up till *now…*

CHARLES. You sure you want to hear this?

FIONA. Positive.

CHARLES. Okay, but I warned you. For the past seven years I've worked for Robert Bruce, magnate, son-of-a-bitch, and principle developer of your supposed golf course. Do you play, by the way?

FIONA. What?

CHARLES. Golf.

FIONA. Never.

CHARLES. Not at *all?*

FIONA. Not even once.

CHARLES. Why?

FIONA. It never seemed interesting.

CHARLES. So…you're sort of like a *virgin* then. I mean, when it comes it comes to golf.

FIONA. Not just to golf.

CHARLES. …*what?*

FIONA. I mean, I am a virgin in more ways than just that.

CHARLES. But surely you don't mean…

FIONA. But I do.

CHARLES. …*but…*

FIONA. In the *bath…?*

CHARLES. Yes! I mean…well, …I don't want to embarrass you, and we did only go so far, but you certainly did seem to know what you were doing up till there.

FIONA. Guess I have good instincts.

CHARLES. Do you ever!

FIONA. I have been saving myself.

CHARLES. FORGET THE EGGS!

FIONA. You'll need your strength.

CHARLES. *Oh my God…*

FIONA. So you were saying…

CHARLES. About…

FIONA. Your life up till now.

CHARLES. Surely that can wait!

FIONA. I need to hear.

CHARLES. Okay, but this really is embarrassing. As I said, I work for Robert Bruce.

FIONA. In what capacity?

CHARLES. I'm what's called a fixer.

FIONA. And what does that mean?

CHARLES. It means I fix things.

FIONA. Such as...

CHARLES. The messes he leaves behind.

FIONA. And does he do that often?

CHARLES. Always.

FIONA. And are you good at this?

CHARLES. Very. And he pays me so well to keep doing this that I have houses and cars all over the place, even with my divorce, which I'd prefer not to talk about, mostly because, if I do, you will ask me what my wife was like, and I now think I actually never knew, and still don't, and in fact don't even know why I married her, though I suspect there must have been a reason lurking somewhere. Luckily, we had no children. When I get a chance, I like to play golf, ski, go fishing and play tennis, which I am particularly good at. Last year I won our club championship. And I think that about does it.

FIONA. Well that is the saddest story I have ever heard!

CHARLES. ...It *is?*

FIONA. Are you kidding? Oh my God! I can see now why you felt so embarrassed telling it. Oh my poor dear darlin' boy! What can I do? I need to do something fast, and relieve all this pain.

CHARLES. What pain?

FIONA. The pain you are feeling. And probably *have* been for so long you don't even notice it anymore. I know! *Yes!* We'll go to *BED!* How does *that* sound?

CHARLES. Uhhhh, good.

FIONA. Okay, this pulls out into a bed. Here, tug.

(*They tug on the couch. As they do...*)

CHARLES. You really think it was that sad a story?

FIONA. Oh my God. I could weep!

CHARLES. Well we don't want that.

FIONA. No we don't. *There!*

(*It's just become a bed.*)

Okay. Off with the robe.

CHARLES. Right.

(*He takes off his robe, she takes off hers. She jumps into bed. He joins her.*)

FIONA. So if it's all right with you, let's get started.

CHARLES. Good.

FIONA. Now, the first thing you need to know –

CHARLES. Let me guess.

FIONA. You won't be able to. The first thing ya need to know, is that I believe you may have faerie blood in you…

(*silence*)

I'm sorry. Did you not hear that?

CHARLES. No, I did. I'm…just…trying to *absorb* all that. Was it something I did in there?

FIONA. Well yes it was actually. But I had my suspicions before. As did my father.

CHARLES. So you *both* thought this!

FIONA. Yes. Even though you do not have red hair, which often, though not necessarily, is the initial giveaway. No, for us the first clue was that you saw the washerwoman. Next, you survived the hill. Third, you've got that stain, and last, but most important, somethin' happened just now in the tub, whose significance I recognized solely because I am a faerie myself.

CHARLES. Are you!

FIONA. I am.

CHARLES. Funny, you look so *real.*

FIONA. So do you.

CHARLES. You even *feel* real!

FIONA. As do you. This is because we're both in human form.

CHARLES. Ah-hah!

FIONA. Anyway, as a faerie, naturally I'm always on the lookout for other ones.

CHARLES. Do they come here a lot?

FIONA. I'll say!

CHARLES. So this is like sort of a *gathering* spot.

FIONA. It is. It's because of the hill. Particularly on Midsummer Eve. I mean you can't *believe* what goes on up there! In fact that entire week!

CHARLES. That's the high season, is it?

FIONA. *Oh my God!* At the pub? You cannot get a table.

CHARLES. And these "visiting faeries"…forgive me, but…

FIONA. No-no. Please.

CHARLES. Well are they not very *tiny?*

FIONA. Well I suppose.

CHARLES. So when they come *into* the pub, how do you know they've come in?

FIONA. Oh no, no, when they come to us they're in human form.

CHARLES. I see.

FIONA. We couldn't serve 'em otherwise.

CHARLES. Well that certainly makes sense.

FIONA. Anyhow, I now believe you may be the faerie I have been waiting for.

CHARLES. Ah-hah!

FIONA. Every faerie has a promised faerie somewhere else, you see.

CHARLES. I didn't know that.

FIONA. Oh yes. And their life's task is to find this promised *Other.*

CHARLES. And you think I may be yours.

FIONA. I think so. But I'll know for sure after we've made love.

CHARLES. Well that seems fair enough.

FIONA. I sure hope it goes well.

(*pause*)

CHARLES. …what…makes you think it wouldn't?

FIONA. Well I've never done this before.

CHARLES. …right.

FIONA. I take it you have.

CHARLES. I have.

FIONA. Did you like it?

CHARLES. I did.

FIONA. Well then I prob'ly will, too!

CHARLES. …so what exactly happened in there that made you think that I might, you know…

FIONA. Have faerie blood in you.

CHARLES. Yes.

FIONA. Well as I said, we faeries look for signs, and you had one in particular.

CHARLES. Which was…

(*The door opens and her father,* **OLD ANGUS**, *walks in.*)

OLD ANGUS. Knock-knock.

FIONA. Hi, dad!

OLD ANGUS. (*seeing them in bed*) Guess the bath went well.

FIONA. *Did it ever!*

OLD ANGUS. Good, 'cause everything went fine down in town, and no search parties will be comin', so you two can have all the privacy ya want. (*going for a drink*) So, in a nutshell…

FIONA. He's got the faerie blood in him.

OLD ANGUS. *I knew it!*

(*to* **CHARLES**, *cowering now under the blanket:*)

And I'll bet ya never even suspected.

FIONA. I think he's a bit overwhelmed.

OLD ANGUS. Well who can blame him? I'm sorry. You were about to say...

FIONA. I was about to tell him what the key sign was.

OLD ANGUS. Somethin' he obviously needs t' know, or he'll remain skeptical.

FIONA. Right. So, anyway, it happened in the bath. Actually, this is a bit embarrassing.

OLD ANGUS. Pretend I'm not here.

(He sits in an easy chair, drink in hand, ready to listen.)

FIONA. Okay. Well at one point – I can't recall exactly what we were doin' prior – but I suddenly noticed that your thingamabob had risen from the water like a periscope. Do you remember?

CHARLES. I believe I do.

FIONA. And as a kind of test, I gave it a little flick.

CHARLES. I remember that, too.

FIONA. And to my surprise and delight it vibrated in the key of A...like a tuning fork.

CHARLES. And you could hear this.

FIONA. Both hear and feel.

CHARLES. *Through the water!*

FIONA. Right through the water.

OLD ANGUS. That's because she's a faerie!

FIONA. By the way, I vibrate as well.

CHARLES. Do you?

FIONA. In fact I'm vibrating now.

CHARLES. In the same key?

FIONA. Yes, but the amplitude is not as great.

CHARLES. Well this is I think possibly if not definitely, no I'd say definitely, the most amazing evening I have ever spent. What do you have to say to that?

FIONA. This is the most amazing evening *I* have ever spent!

(They kiss. It's a long one. Overwhelms them both.)

CHARLES. *(to* **OLD ANGUS**, *barely able to breathe)* And are you a faerie, too?

OLD ANGUS. Oh no! No, just she.

CHARLES. So then I guess your *wife* must have been the, uh, …

OLD ANGUS. No-no. No, my wife, may she rest in peace, was like me.

FIONA. I was adopted.

CHARLES. *Adopted!*

OLD ANGUS. It's her *folks* who were the faeries.

CHARLES. And they just *gave* her to you?

OLD ANGUS. Yes.

CHARLES. …*Recently?*

OLD ANGUS. No-no. When she was a wee bairn.

CHARLES. And what sort of form was she in?

OLD ANGUS. This.

CHARLES. *Human!*

OLD ANGUS. Yes.

FIONA. But not as big.

CHARLES. No, I understand. So how'd you know she was a faerie? Not that I'm doubting you.

OLD ANGUS. Well her folks told me.

CHARLES. You *saw* them!

OLD ANGUS. No, they left a note.

CHARLES. On…

OLD ANGUS. Her bassinet.

CHARLES. "Take care of this faerie child."

OLD ANGUS. Something like that.

CHARLES. And why do you suppose they did this?

OLD ANGUS. Well they knew I was in grief.

CHARLES. *Grief?*

OLD ANGUS. Well my wife had just died, and our little child along with her, and I was…*desolate* I guess you'd say. And the faeries noticed this. They're all around us, you see. They look *out* for us. And so, as a kind of *gift,* to assuage my grief, they gave me *her*, to raise as my own, and she's been my precious lamb, and indeed my life, ever since.

CHARLES. ...well that is an extraordinary story.

OLD ANGUS. It is indeed.

(**CHARLES**, *unsure of what to say to that, decides to say nothing and just lies there. After a while, the lights fade.*)

Scene 2

(The next day. A meadow outside of town…)

(and then…)

(We hear a bagpipe. It's getting closer. Enter, a procession, some men in kilts, one of them the culprit playing the bagpipes.)

(Among the others are **OLD ANGUS, REVEREND HAGGLEHORNE, MACKENZIE STEWART, LITTLE NICK, HARRY MORGAN,** *and* **FELICITY.***)*

(The reason for this gathering is soon apparent. It's **ROSS,** *who is presently rolled on [or carried, doesn't really matter] sitting bolt upright in an open coffin.)*

(At the proper moment, and in just the right place — that being the spot commanding the finest vista — they set his casket down. And the music stops. For a few moments, everyone watches **ROSS,** *taking in the view, overwhelmed. Finally, when he can speak…)*

ROSS. Look a' all that, will ya? Just look…

(They all look.)

Takes a tragedy like this to bring it all int' perspective. I see it now. This fair island is my true luve. And if I have ever wronged ya in any way, I do beg your forgiveness. Though I suspect it's too late. So be it. I accept my fate. But oh my God, I will miss ya so… *(begins to recite) As fair art thou, my bonnie lass!*

MACKENZIE STEWART. Willy, it's all right.

ROSS. *(undeterred) So deep in luve am I…*

MACKENZIE STEWART. Really, man. We admire Rabbie Burns as much as you, but we're on a schedule here, ya see.

ROSS. *And I will luve thee still, my dear,*
Till a' the seas gang dry.

*(***ROSS,** *feeling inspired, rises up to his full height.)*

ROSS. *(cont.) And fare thee weel, my only luve,*
And fare thee weel, a while!
And I will come again, my luve,
Tho' it were ten thousand mile.

MACKENZIE STEWART. Willy, I hafta say, for a man who's about to die, I don't think I've ever seen ya lookin' better.

ROSS. Looks can be deceivin'.

REVEREND HAGGLEHORNE. But they can't deceive the Lord!

ROSS. Who invited him?

MACKENZIE STEWART. All right. Enuff. Sit back down and let's just git on with it.

(**ROSS** *sits back down. Whereupon* **MACKENZIE STEWART** *gives a signal, and the bagpiper begins playing "Will Ye No Come Back Again?" After a few bars, singing commences.*)

VARIOUS SINGERS.
WILLIAM ROSS IS GO'N AWAY,
MAY HIS LIFE NA END IN VAIN;
MONY A HEART WILL BREAK IN TWAY,
SHOULD HE NE'ER COME BACK AGAIN.

ALL.
WILL YE NO COME BACK AGAIN?
WILL YE NO COME BACK AGAIN?
BETTER LO'ED YE CANNA BE.
WILL YE NO COME BACK AGAIN?

(Now it's **ROSS**'s *turn.)*

ROSS. *(through his tears)*
SWEET THE BLUEBIRD'S NOTE DIDST HANG,
LILTING WILDLY UP THE GLEN;
AND AYE THE O'ERWORLD O' I SANG,
"COULD I PLEASE COME BACK AGAIN?"

ALL.
COULD HE PLEASE COME BACK AGAIN?
COULD HE PLEASE COME BACK AGAIN?

BETTER LO'ED YE CANNA BE,
COULD HE PLEASE COME BACK AGAIN?

(And with that, the music ends.)

MACKENZIE STEWART. I would be lyin' if I didn't tell ya that if anythin', you actually seem to be gettin' stronger.

ROSS. I just don't understand it.

LITTLE NICK. Wait-a-second! Maybe that American didn't really *see* the washerwoman, but someone *else!* Who just happened to be *holdin'* a washboard.

ROSS. But he distinctly said she was carrying my shirt.

MACKENZIE STEWART. Yes, but modesty aside, it's a nice shirt, Willy. Maybe someone had it duplicated. *Where is that American? (to* **OLD ANGUS***)* You said he stayed with you last night.

OLD ANGUS. Aye, but he'll be here.

LITTLE NICK. What was he doin' with you?

OLD ANGUS. He got lost in the woods. But luckily, I found 'm and brought him in to dry, and he was so exhausted, poor lamb, he fell asleep while dryin' out.

MACKENZIE STEWART. Well he'd best come soon, he's got a lot to answer for.

LITTLE NICK. Here he comes! And with your daughter yet!

(**CHARLES** *enters with* **FIONA**, *both looking uncommonly happy.)*

CHARLES. Good morrow, fair citizens of Muckle Skerry!

MACKENZIE STEWART. And a good morrow back t' you, Mr. Pearse! Tell me, did ya have a good night's sleep, snicker-snicker?

OLD ANGUS. You watch your tongue!

MACKENZIE STEWART. But did he watch his?

OLD ANGUS. That's my daughter you're referrin' to!

MACKENZIE STEWART. I know, and that's a young man, and just look at 'em both. If they was grinnin' any wider, their cheeks 'ud split. (And at a funeral yet!) *A question, Mr. Pearse!* That is, if ya can take yer mind off that young red-headed girl. I know it ain't easy; we try all the time, and still can't manage it.

OLD ANGUS. *WHAT'S YER BLOODY QUESTION!?*

MACKENZIE STEWART. Did ya really see the washerwoman or did ya not? Think carefully.

CHARLES. I did.

MACKENZIE STEWART. Then why isn't he dead yet?

ROSS. It makes no sense.

MACKENZIE STEWART. Maybe if we all concentrate…

LITTLE NICK. QUIET IN BACK!

MACKENZIE STEWART. WE'RE GONNA CONCENTRATE ON WILLY'S DEATH!

(*They all quiet down and concentrate,* **ROSS** *included.* **FELICITY,** *taking advantage of the lull, sidles up to* **CHARLES.**)

FELICITY. Could I talk to you a moment?

CHARLES. Oh! Yes. Of course. *So how'd it go up there?*

FELICITY. Worse that I could ever have imagined, better than I could've hoped. First the good part. It would seem my theory is correct. Something transcendentally erotic is definitely going on up there. The bad part? I didn't stay long enough to know for sure.
Oh Mr. Pearse, please don't think ill of me, but there I was, nearly at the top, when all at once the ground began to shake, and I thought, oh my God, it's happening! And then I will see. And finally I will *know!* But then, suddenly I got so frightened that I turned and ran down the hill. Can you believe it? After all these years, I finally had my chance, and I ran away like a bloody coward!

CHARLES. Yes, well it sounds like you were scared.

FELICITY. Of *course* I was scared! I just TOLD you I was!

CHARLES. Yes, but if it was as scary as you *say*…

FELICITY. You know what? Just forget it. My mistake! Somehow, I thought that when you heard what I went through up there last night, somehow you'd want to go back up there with me. Obviously I was wrong! Clearly it takes a very special kind of person to understand these kinds of things, and clearly you're just not that kind of person.

(**FELICITY** *walks off.* **OLD ANGUS** *immediately takes her place.*)

OLD ANGUS. *(sotto voce)* In case you're wonderin', I've told no one.

CHARLES. About…

OLD ANGUS. *Everything.*

(**OLD ANGUS** *moves away.* **CHARLES** *stares after him.* **HARRY MORGAN** *moves in.*)

HARRY MORGAN. Guess who's on his way.

CHARLES. No idea.

HARRY MORGAN. Who is the last person you would like to see right now?

CHARLES. *How?*

HARRY MORGAN. In a helicopter. It just landed on the heath.

CHARLES. *Oh my God…*

ONE OF THE OTHERS. Why didn't we hear it land?

CHARLES. *(glumly)* Stealth technology.

LITTLE NICK. It's him all right! I recognize 'm from his photos!

(**MACKENZIE STEWART** *gives a signal, and they begin to sing that famous old song, "Sumer is Icumen In," but with a different lyric.*)

ALL.
ROBERT-THE-BRUCE IS CUMMIN HERE!
LHUDI SING CUCCU.
BLESS THE SOD WHICH HE DOTH TROD,
AND SPRINGETH WE ANEW.
SING CUCCU!
SING CUCCU!

(And so on, in round form, until they are interrupted by the man himself, entering like a colossus. The music stops.)

ROBERT BRUCE. Well I'm not quite sure about that cuckoo thing, but the effort is much appreciated. I had thought my arrival would surprise you, but it would seem someone warned you I was coming.

MACKENZIE STEWART. Actually, no sir. But we always figured you'd be coming *some* day, so we've been practicin'.

ROBERT BRUCE. Good for you. *Ross!* What the hell're you doing in a coffin?

ROSS. It's a long story.

ROBERT BRUCE. Well you can tell me later.

ROSS. Unless I'm dead by then.

ROBERT BRUCE. Well then someone else will. Now where is Pearse?

CHARLES. Over here!

ROBERT BRUCE. Where the hell's your phone?

CHARLES. Lightning struck it.

ROBERT BRUCE. Well then how the hell was I supposed to reach you? I should charge you for the fuel. *Morgan!* There you are! Stop hiding! Now what the hell's going on?

HARRY MORGAN. Simply put, we cannot build a golf course here.

ROBERT BRUCE. Is that some sort of joke?

HARRY MORGAN. I'm afraid not. Though this next part may seem like one. The reason we cannot build it here is because of the faeries who (apparently) live directly underneath our proposed 18th green. Pearse will back me up on this.

ROBERT BRUCE. WHAT!

HARRY MORGAN. I know. It's a bit of a stunner. However! All is not lost. You do have several options. For instance, we could proceed as planned, and build the course. Apparently, the faeries don't mind if we do.

It's *playing* on it that's the problem. To do *that*, you need a schedule. Which unfortunately only the faeries seem to possess. Give him an example.

MACKENZIE STEWART. Well today, for instance, one could not tee off at all.

ROBERT BRUCE. And why is that?

MACKENZIE STEWART. Well because today happens to be the first Sunday after a full moon. So that explains that. Thursdays now – those I'm afraid are out altogether. On the other hand, Wednesdays are fine, unless it's a *leap* year, in which case the second Wednesday after Shrove *Tuesday* –

ROBERT BRUCE. Excuse me, but whose land is this?

MACKENZIE STEWART. What do you mean?

ROBERT BRUCE. I mean WHOSE FUCKING LAND IS THIS, YOURS OR MINE?

MACKENZIE STEWART. There's no need to shout.

ROBERT BRUCE. I AM NOT SHOUTING! *(to* **CHARLES**, *louder still) TELL HIM!*

CHARLES. Mr. Bruce does not shout.

ROBERT BRUCE. *IS THAT CLEAR!?*

MACKENZIE STEWART. Yessir, my mistake. Could you repeat the question? But maybe even more softly than before.

ROBERT BRUCE. *Whose fucking land is this, yours or mine?*

MACKENZIE STEWART. Right. Well, first, let me say that I do not mean this as an insult, because we are all deeply honored by what you've done for us so far, and we hope will keep doing, but, according to Scottish common law, as it's been interpreted, or at least as I *understand* it –

ROBERT BRUCE. MORGAN!

HARRY MORGAN. Sir!

ROBERT BRUCE. Is this my land or not? Yes or no.

HARRY MORGAN. No.

ROBERT BRUCE. PEARSE!

CHARLES. Sir!

ROBERT BRUCE. SAME QUESTION!

CHARLES. Well that's a tricky one.

ROBERT BRUCE. *MORGAN!*

HARRY MORGAN. Sir!

ROBERT BRUCE. In your opinion, was that a tricky question?

HARRY MORGAN. Not at all.

ROBERT BRUCE. *(to* **CHARLES***)* So is this my land or not? Let's have it. Yes or no?

CHARLES. Well before I got here I would have definitely said yes.

ROBERT BRUCE. And *now?*

CHARLES. I'd have to say it may be a bit of both.

ROBERT BRUCE. That is unacceptable.

CHARLES. Then I'm afraid I must agree with Mr. Morgan. *No.*

ROBERT BRUCE. Okay. I see what's happening. And I don't like it, so here is the deal. Listen carefully. This may sound at first like a game but I promise you it's not. Here it goes. Ready? Good. So! I say this is *my* land. Now, who here disagrees?

(Hands shoot up everywhere, **ROSS***'s included.* **ROBERT BRUCE** *takes it all in.)*

So then we'll just have to work this out. Pearse!

CHARLES. Sir!

ROBERT BRUCE. Work it out.

CHARLES. In what sense?

ROBERT BRUCE. In the sense that I want it absolutely understood by one and all that is my land. You look hesitant.

CHARLES. Probably because I'm not sure how to go about what you just asked.

ROBERT BRUCE. That is what I pay you for. Now go and figure it out.

CHARLES. Right.

ROBERT BRUCE. And I want it done by the time Mr. Morgan and I get back.

HARRY MORGAN. From where?

ROBERT BRUCE. Playing golf. Who here has a set of clubs?

(Hands rise.)

I'll want one set for Mr. Morgan, and one for me.

MACKENZIE STEWART. Excuse me.

ROBERT BRUCE. Oh. Sorry. That's right. You said we can't *play* today! Well fuck you, fuck the moon, and fuck the faeries. This is my fucking land, I paid for it, and now I can fucking well do whatever I want with it. Where did you say these faeries live?

HARRY MORGAN. Up there.

ROBERT BRUCE. Where our 18th green's supposed to go.

HARRY MORGAN. Exactly. Or…to be even *more* precise…

MACKENZIE STEWART. Under the rock.

ROBERT BRUCE. What rock?

HARRY MORGAN. The one that's in the middle of our…

ROBERT BRUCE. 18th green?

*(**HARRY MORGAN** nods.)*

Well, faeries or not, we obviously need to move it, don't we?

MACKENZIE STEWART. Except you can't.

ROBERT BRUCE. Would you like to bet?

MACKENZIE STEWART. No, sir. Because that would not be fair, as I know you would lose.

ROBERT BRUCE. Would I? Tell you what: why don't we see? Harry, when we're finished playing, call your office and have them send down some dynamite, enough say to blow up a mountain top, and let's see how the rock and those faeries fare after that. Now, who's getting us our clubs?

MACKENZIE STEWART. …*Nick?*

LITTLE NICK. Are you really sure?

MACKENZIE STEWART. Absolutely. Mr. Bruce wishes to play golf. Who are we to say no?

LITTLE NICK. ...Right. Won't take but a moment.

(**LITTLE NICK** *rushes off.*)

ROBERT BRUCE. Pearse!

CHARLES. Sir!

ROBERT BRUCE. We'll need a caddy.

CHARLES. But what about...

ROBERT BRUCE. The dynamite? No-no, Harry's taking care of that.

CHARLES. No, I mean...well you just gave me this *task*.

ROBERT BRUCE. *What* task?

CHARLES. About, you know, the *land*. How to, somehow, *prove*...

ROBERT BRUCE. That I actually own it?

CHARLES. Yes.

ROBERT BRUCE. What, you can't think while you caddy? What's the big deal? You carry our bags, you call out the yardage, and you *think!*

CHARLES. Well I suppose I can do that.

ROBERT BRUCE. Of course you can. That's why you work for me!

HARRY MORGAN. Excuse me. But would you mind if I had a word with Mr. Pearse? It won't take but a moment.

(**BRUCE** *signals acquiescence.* **HARRY MORGAN** *pulls* **CHARLES** *aside.*)

Do not come up.

CHARLES. What do you mean?

HARRY MORGAN. I mean, there is some unfinished business between Mr. Bruce and myself, which I need to deal with, but you do not. For yer own sake, *stay down here.*

(**HARRY MORGAN** *gives* **CHARLES** *a look that says, I mean it,* then walks back, **CHARLES** *staring after him, stunned.*)

ROBERT BRUCE. *Pearse?*

> (*But* **CHARLES** *is still thinking about what* **HARRY MORGAN** *just said.*)

> …PEARSE!

CHARLES. What?

ROBERT BRUCE. Let's get moving!

CHARLES. Oh…right.

FIONA. He's not going up.

CHARLES. *Fiona!*

FIONA. No. I can handle it.

ROBERT BRUCE. Who is this?

OLD ANGUS. My daughter.

ROBERT BRUCE. And who the hell is he?

FIONA. My father.

CHARLES. Fiona, *please!*

FIONA. No, trust me, I can handle this. *(to Bruce)* The reason he is not going up with you is because, for one thing, no one is supposed to play up there today, *and that includes caddying.* But even *more* important –

CHARLES. *This is not the place!*

FIONA. *He needs to know!*

ROBERT BRUCE. Know what?

FIONA. That he is a faerie himself!

> (*stunned silence everywhere*)

> Now, at first glance you might think, well if he's one o' them, can't *he* go up? He can indeed. *BUT NOT WITH GOLF CLUBS!*

CHARLES. Okay, first of all…

ROBERT BRUCE. No, let me talk. When she says faerie, I assume she means…

CHARLES. The kind who live up there.

ROBERT BRUCE. Well that's a relief. *(to* **FIONA***)* So you think he lives up there.

FIONA. No-no.

OLD ANGUS. He's an *off*-island faerie.

ROBERT BRUCE. I see. And how exactly did you determine this, if you don't mind my asking?

FIONA. Well, I am a faerie myself, and I can sense these things!

ROBERT BRUCE. Did anyone *else* here know this?

MACKENZIE STEWART. About him or about her?

ROBERT BRUCE. Either one.

MACKENZIE STEWART. Well we've been suspecting it about her, but him, no that is a surprise.

ROBERT BRUCE. *(to them all)* DO YOU TAKE ME FOR AN ASS!? *(to* **MACKENZIE STEWART***) Where are those fucking clubs?*

(enter, **LITTLE NICK***, on the run, golf bags slung over his shoulders)*

LITTLE NICK. HERE THEY ARE! And I've given ya some extra balls. (You're gonna need 'em up there.)

ROBERT BRUCE. PEARSE! GRAB THOSE BAGS!

CHARLES. No.

ROBERT BRUCE. *What?*

CHARLES. No! I am not going. And it's not because of anything she just said. Yes, it's true, she thinks I am a faerie, and that she is too, and who can say we're not? I mean for sure. I mean is there a God? Is Fiona a faerie? It's like that.

No, the reason I'm staying down here is because, because, *because*…I do not like caddying, and never have. In fact, I don't even like golf. And so *no*. In fact – yes why not? I quit. I hereby quit. Because…here it comes! *(I can't believe it!)* BECAUSE…

I am in love with her. You hear that? I am in love with her! FAERIE OR NOT, I AM IN LOVE WITH HER! I mean, who wouldn't be? Well I am.

*(***CHARLES*** turns and stares at* **FIONA***, overwhelmed by what he has just said. Its impact has only just hit him. Then something else occurs to him.)*

(struggling to take his eyes off **FIONA***)* Plus...*plus...*

(He turns to **ROBERT BRUCE** *again, but this time with newfound strength. This is a new man talking!)*

I don't like *you.* In fact, I never have. In fact, *no* one has. In fact, no one *does.* And, unless I miss my guess, no one ever will!

ROSS. I AM COMIN' BACK T' LIFE!

CHARLES. I wasn't done.

ROSS. Sorry.

CHARLES. That wasn't fair. Clearly there must be *some* good things about you, else why would I have stayed with you so long? I've never understood it. Unfortunately, right now I can't think of one. But if I do, you'll be the first to know.

(And with that, he goes back to staring at **FIONA***, and she, at him. If this weren't real love, this would be sickening, but it is real love, and everyone there knows it,* **ROBERT BRUCE** *included.)*

ROBERT BRUCE. *(finally; though still clearly seething)* So who wants to caddy?

FELICITY. I will!

ROBERT BRUCE. Who're you?

FELICITY. Felicity Oliphant, British Museum, and an expert on the Bog People.

ROBERT BRUCE. The *what?*

HARRY MORGAN. You don't want to go into it.

ROBERT BRUCE. Well, if you think you're up to it. *(to* **CHARLES***)* I'll deal with you later.

*(***FELICITY** *picks up their golf bags and off they go.)*

(to **HARRY MORGAN***, as they leave)* By the way, what's your handicap?

HARRY MORGAN. *You.*

(exit the two golfers and their caddy, heading for the hill)

MACKENZIE STEWART. QUICK! TO THE BOATS!

(They all rush off, opposite direction from the golfers.)

ROSS. I can't believe it! They're leaving me here t' die! Well fuck this! I'M COMIN' WITH YA! *Wouldn't miss this fer the world! (***ROSS*** climbs out of his coffin.)* Reverend? Why don't you come, too? Who knows? Might do ya some good.

REVEREND HAGGLEHORNE. Why not? *(to the heavens)* I meant it, Lord. *Any parish but this!*

(Exit, **ROSS,** *re-vitalized,* **REVEREND HAGGLEHORNE** *tagging along behind, looking lost.)*

CHARLES. Where are they all going?

OLD ANGUS. Out to sea.

FIONA. It's the only good vantage point. *(re the hill)* If ya wanna see what's happening' up there.

OLD ANGUS. They'll hafta use binoculars.

FIONA. Yes, but at least they'll be safe.

OLD ANGUS. I'm not sure. *Here it comes.*

CHARLES. What?

FIONA. The storm.

CHARLES. I don't see anything.

OLD ANGUS. You will.

FIONA. Yes, but it'll be strictly localized. No, they should be fine out there. And as long we stay down here, we should be too.

OLD ANGUS. Still, wouldn't hurt to take shelter.

FIONA. You're prob'ly right. *(to* **CHARLES***)* One never knows.

(They start to leave, expecting **CHARLES** *to follow. But he doesn't.)*

CHARLES. One second. That is, if you don't mind…

(They stop and stare at him, unsure of what he means.)

(gazing out) I just want to look.

(Now they understand.)

It's really beautiful, isn't it?

OLD ANGUS. It is indeed.

(**CHARLES** *continue to drink it all in.*)

CHARLES. What's that called? Out there…

OLD ANGUS. What?

CHARLES. That low hedge running through that field, the one with all those sheep.

OLD ANGUS. A low hedge.

CHARLES. Ah…and that clump of trees, up past the sheep?

OLD ANGUS. We call that a clump o' trees.

CHARLES. I mean, what kind are they?

FIONA. Rowan, prob'ly.

OLD ANGUS. Maybe some juniper.

CHARLES. And over there?

FIONA. Those are bay willows.

CHARLES. And those shimmering blue things?

OLD ANGUS. Bluebells.

FIONA. It's the season.

CHARLES. Well it's all just sort of amazing, isn't it?

OLD ANGUS. Indeed it is.

(*In the distance, a low, ominous rumble of thunder is heard.*)

FIONA. I think we'd best get a move on.

OLD ANGUS. I think yer right. (*to* **CHARLES**, *still staring out*) Worry not. It's like this all around. There's no one special place.

(*Exit, all,* **CHARLES** *looking around in awe as they go. As they do,* another *rumble of the thunder is heard, this one noticeably louder than the previous.*)

(*Then, as if from nowhere, a tremendous bolt of lightning tears through the sky.*)

(*Darkness falls. A roll of thunder follows. As it subsides, dappled light breaks through the storm clouds to reveal…*)

A Rocky Crag Up the Side of the "Forbidden Hill"

(The **WASHERWOMAN** *stands, almost magically, on the crag, stringing up a laundry line in the building wind. On a rising twist of air, we can make out her voice as she sings.)*

WASHERWOMAN. *(eerily)*
THREE WENT UP
AND THREE STAYED DOWN
BUT ONLY THREE
OF 'EM WILL DROWN.
THE EARTH IS THE SEA AND THE SEA 'THE EARTH
WHEN FAIRIES JUDGE A HUMAN'S WORTH.

(She hangs three shirts onto the line, like prayer flags in the wind. They are, noticeably, the shirts of: **ROBERT BRUCE**, **HARRY MORGAN**, *and* **FELICITY**.*)*

YES, THREE WENT UP
AND THREE STAYED DOWN
BUT ONLY THREE
RETURN TO TOWN.

THE SEA IS THE EARTH AND THE EARTH 'THE SEA
WHEN HUMANS HURT A FAIRY FREE.

(And with this incantation, things will never be the same again.)

(A brief moment of calm. The **WASHERWOMAN** *looks to the sky, then, catching us off guard with its impossibly loud light: lightning strikes once more.)*

(And with that the scene shifts to…)

The Edge of a Grassy Plateau

(High above town, the peak of the "Forbidden Hill" rising in the distance. The ominous sound of thunder we just heard is still rumbling. The storm is getting closer.)

(Enter, **ROBERT BRUCE** *and* **HARRY MORGAN** *through grass so tall it nearly reaches their hips,* **FELICITY** *behind them with their golf bags, furled umbrella sticking out of one.)*

HARRY MORGAN. You sure you wouldn't rather play tomorrow?

ROBERT BRUCE. Can't bear losing, can you?

HARRY MORGAN. It has nothing to do with that. It's that storm that troubles me.

ROBERT BRUCE. What storm?

HARRY MORGAN. The one heading our way.

ROBERT BRUCE. We have an umbrella.

HARRY MORGAN. Yes, but what if there's lightning?

ROBERT BRUCE. She holds up the umbrella, and we go somewhere else. *(to* **FELICITY***)* Just kidding. *(to* **HARRY MORGAN***) She thinks I'm kidding. (to* **FELICITY***)* Now where's my ball?

FELICITY. No idea.

ROBERT BRUCE. Where's his?

FELICITY. No idea.

ROBERT BRUCE. Well then fuck this. Here's what we're going to do. We're going to play out there, where the grass is shorter.

FELICITY. That's the bog.

ROBERT BRUCE. Well then that's where we're going. Oh God, I am happy today! And do you know why? Because of that hill.

HARRY MORGAN. Where the faeries live.

ROBERT BRUCE. Not for long. Anyway, I was up there once. Did you know that?

HARRY MORGAN. I did.

ROBERT BRUCE. That's right, of course you did. Greatest day I ever spent! What a spot! And the *view*... Unbelievable. And that *girl* I was with! *Talk about a view!* Wonder what became of her...

(*Suddenly,* **FELICITY** *rushes ahead.*)

Where the hell are *you* going?

FELICITY. Top o' the hill!

ROBERT BRUCE. You're a caddy. You're supposed to stay *behind* us.

FELICITY. (*gesturing to the summit*) Well then hit *that* way.

ROBERT BRUCE. You've never done this before, have you?

FELICITY. No.

(*Exit all, toward the bog and the hill,* **FELICITY** *slouching along behind.*)

(*More thunder heard. The storm is definitely getting closer.*)

(*A sudden flash of lightning blinds us briefly! When the lightning passes, we are no longer on the hill, but...*)

On A Path Below the Hill

(The sound of thunder is muffled down here, the side of the hill serving as both a shelter and a baffle.)

(Enter **OLD ANGUS, CHARLES** *and* **FIONA,** *talking as they go.)*

CHARLES. So, assuming we get married, …won't you miss all this?

FIONA. Why would I miss this?

CHARLES. Well we'd have to move to New York.

FIONA. *(stunned, horrified)* New *York?*

OLD ANGUS. Let me handle this. *(to* **CHARLES***; just as horrified)* New *York?*

CHARLES. Well yes. I mean, that's where I live.

OLD ANGUS. Not if you marry her. No, you've got to live on Muckle Skerry.

CHARLES. Full *time?*

OLD ANGUS. Pretty much. Though ya can go off now and then, but why would ya want to?

CHARLES. Because New York is where I work.

FIONA. I thought you just gave that up.

CHARLES. No, it's the *job* I gave up. I didn't give up *working!*

FIONA. Well you could do something *here.*

CHARLES. Like what?

OLD ANGUS. Be a fisherman.

FIONA. You could help dad!

CHARLES. Except there are no fish.

OLD ANGUS. Well maybe they'll come back!

FIONA. Maybe you'll even *bring* them back. We like you. Maybe the fish will too.

CHARLES. Okay, forget the job part. So! Assuming we are married now, and…living here…

OLD ANGUS. Now you're talkin'!

CHARLES. What are the chances I will wake one morning and –

OLD ANGUS. Find she's sprouted wings? None at all.

CHARLES. And why is that?

FIONA. Because when a faerie's born in human form, she *stays* that way.

CHARLES. You see, that's something I didn't know.

OLD ANGUS. How could you?

CHARLES. And what about all those *other* faeries? The ones you say visit here? Are they *all* like that?

OLD ANGUS. Oh no!

FIONA. Most o' them are only *temporarily* in human form.

OLD ANGUS. Faeries can move in and out at will, ya see.

FIONA. But it's dangerous.

OLD ANGUS. If they don't know what they're doin', faeries are easily seduced up here.

FIONA. And then, before they know it, they are trapped.

OLD ANGUS. Let me give you an example. About ten years before Fiona blessed my life, a young faerie girl – or so the story goes – became enamored of the human world, and began spending as much time as she could in human form. And to help her get along, chose the name Sally. Why "Sally"? No idea. But it's a nice name, and that's what she chose.

(Exit all. As they go…)

(The muffled sound of rolling thunder is heard, sound growing stronger and more ominous as the scene shifts to…)

The Hill, Once Again

*(But this time we're farther uphill. This is the bog. Enter, Bruce and Morgan, slogging their way across it, searching for their golf balls, **FELICITY** just behind.)*

(The summit of the "Forbidden Hill" looms up ahead.)

HARRY MORGAN. *(as they go)* So you really don't remember her…

ROBERT BRUCE. Who?

HARRY MORGAN. That girl you screwed *right up there.*

ROBERT BRUCE. Oh, *that* one. What was her name again?

HARRY MORGAN. Sally.

ROBERT BRUCE. Right, Sally. How the hell did you remember that?

(They disappear around a rocky promontory. As they do, we go back down to …)

Another Part of the Path

(Enter **OLD ANGUS** *followed by* **FIONA** *and* **CHARLES**, *hand-in-hand.)*

OLD ANGUS. Anyway, if the story's true – and I tend to think it is – it is possible (not definite, but possible) that during one of Sally's "day trips in human form", she met young Mr. Harry Morgan – *yes, that very one!* – who of course would not have known she was a faerie, as you'd have to be one yerself to know.

FIONA. I'm sorry. Why are you telling him this?

OLD ANGUS. Well, I just thought –

FIONA. What happens is so *sad!*

OLD ANGUS. You're right. Way too sad. Forget I said anything.

CHARLES. No, please, I want to know!

(exit all)

(The thunder is growing even louder.)

Back on the "Forbidden Hill"

(The summit has gotten a lot closer, as has the storm. Sky turning an eerily ominous color. One has rarely seen sky like this, if ever.)

(enter **ROBERT BRUCE, MORGAN,** *and* **FELICITY***)*

ROBERT BRUCE. In *love* with her!

HARRY MORGAN. Yes.

ROBERT BRUCE. Okay, stop right here. How the hell could you have been in love with her when you didn't even *know* the girl?

HARRY MORGAN. Then how come I knew her name?

ROBERT BRUCE. Because I *told* you it!

HARRY MORGAN. No, I told *you!* I was the one who MET her!

ROBERT BRUCE. Okay, fine. For argument's sake, let's suppose you met her first. If she was even *half* as good as I personally know she was, why would you have even *mentioned* her to me?

HARRY MORGAN. Because you were my friend, and I was in love with her, and I didn't know what to do.

ROBERT BRUCE. Wait. It's beginning to come back.

HARRY MORGAN. Ah-hah!

ROBERT BRUCE. So how'd you know I fucked her?

HARRY MORGAN. You TOLD me you did!

ROBERT BRUCE. Why would I do that?

HARRY MORGAN. Because you were PROUD of it!

ROBERT BRUCE. Okay. Now it's coming back. So what became of her?

HARRY MORGAN. She got pregnant.

ROBERT BRUCE. How'd you know?

HARRY MORGAN. People told me.

ROBERT BRUCE. What people?

HARRY MORGAN. In her village. One day I decided to go back and find her and apologize for not having *protected* her from you.

ROBERT BRUCE. Where was I?

HARRY MORGAN. You'd gone back to the States by then.

ROBERT BRUCE. Let me tell you something about that girl…

HARRY MORGAN. She was *innocent!*

ROBERT BRUCE. Obviously you didn't know her the way I did.

HARRY MORGAN. No, I knew her better.

ROBERT BRUCE. Ho-ho-ho.

HARRY MORGAN. That girl did not know what she was *doing!*

ROBERT BRUCE. Oh didn't she?

HARRY MORGAN. No! Or at least not on *your* sordid level. And probably not even mine. Which is why I'd stopped seeing her.

ROBERT BRUCE. That is so fucked up.

HARRY MORGAN. So I went back, but couldn't find her anywhere, and when I described her, people said she'd had a child, a boy, from some affair she'd had, and run away in disgrace with her little boy to America, hoping to find his father, who she believed *loved* her, because he'd *told* her he did just before he took her knickers down.

ROBERT BRUCE. That doesn't sound like me.

HARRY MORGAN. Right. Let me tell you something. This golf course here, which you propose to build, will not happen, *cannot* happen, and never could, which is why we went into it with you.

ROBERT BRUCE. What the hell are you talking about?

HARRY MORGAN. About three years ago we had a slight financial crunch brought on by a colossal blunder courtesy of one William Ross, which I'm sure we could've gotten out of, but not easily. But then, as Fate would have it, my long-seated and simmering hatred of you bubbled forth. "Eureka!" I declared. "Let us develop a golf course on Muckle Skerry!" "But you can't," my partners said. "They believe in faeries there, and they'll never let ya build! "I know," I said. "But Robert Bruce does *not.*"

ROBERT BRUCE. What's your name again?

FELICITY. Felicity.

ROBERT BRUCE. Felicity, hand me a 5 iron, would you?

HARRY MORGAN. All we needed was enough from you to bail us out, plus a little extra for our efforts, and your twenty million more than covered that. By the way, we did not know about the Bog People then, just the faeries, which was enough. The Bog People simply brought things to a head a bit sooner. No big deal; one way or another, it was all goin' down, with Ross *seemingly* the culprit – a role he vehemently resisted. (But he had no choice.) But then, we knew he'd be fine, as would we, because clearly you would never sue. Way too embarrssing! No, you are fucked, Mr. Robert Bruce. You've no idea how long I've waited to say those blessed words.

(ROBERT BRUCE *attacks* **HARRY MORGAN** *with his 5 iron.)*

(HARRY MORGAN *runs uphill,* **ROBERT BRUCE** *chasing after him,* **FELICITY** *chasing after them both.)*

(The storm is almost on them now!)

(Meanwhile, down below…)

Same Path, Farther Along

(**OLD ANGUS**, **FIONA** *and* **CHARLES** *enter*)

OLD ANGUS. Anyway, there you have it.

CHARLES. Was the father Harry Morgan?

OLD ANGUS. No-no.

FIONA. Rumor has it that it was some American.

OLD ANGUS. But no one knows for sure.

CHARLES. *Oh my God…*

OLD ANGUS. So who were your folks?

CHARLES. I don't know. I was adopted. *Be right back!*

(**CHARLES** *races off and up the hill.*)

OLD ANGUS. *Adopted!*

FIONA. I knew it!

(*They run after him.*)

(*As they do, we move upwards with them, but a lot faster, all the way to…*)

The Summit

(It's a storm like no other. Lear never faced anything even remotely like this!)

(Enter, **ROBERT BRUCE***, still wielding his five iron, battling the wind,* **FELICITY** *just behind him, having just as hard a time.)*

ROBERT BRUCE. MORGAN! Which way did he go?

FELICITY. I thought it was this way!

ROBERT BRUCE. Well I don't see him! *Oh no...*

FELICITY. What?

ROBERT BRUCE. I think I'm sinking...I am! *Oh my God...*

FELICITY. Here, give me your hand.

ROBERT BRUCE. Thank you.

    *(***FELICITY** *pulls him out.)*

Talk about hazards...

FELICITY. One needs to tread carefully up here.

ROBERT BRUCE. I'll say. Now where the hell is he? *Oh my God...*

    (He's just started sinking again. Once more she helps him out.)

FELICITY. Come, we'll go together, I've been here before.

ROBERT BRUCE. And you've come *back?*

FELICITY. Actually, I love it up here.

ROBERT BRUCE. What's your name again?

FELICITY. Felicity.

ROBERT BRUCE. Well Felicity, you are one helluva caddy, let me tell you.

    (Hand-in-hand, they move on, fighting a wind so strong they walk at a forty-five degree angle, and even so hardly make progress.)

HARRY MORGAN'S VOICE. *I'm over here!*

ROBERT BRUCE. Harry?

HARRY MORGAN'S VOICE. *To your right!*

ROBERT BRUCE. I can't see you!

HARRY MORGAN'S VOICE. I know! Just a few steps more! You're doing great!

(**ROBERT BRUCE** *does as bid.*)

There!

(**ROBERT BRUCE** *screams. That's because* **HARRY MORGAN**, *who has sunk up to his chest in the ground, has just grabbed Bruce by the ankle.*)

(*Now he's trying to pulls Bruce in with him.*)

(*Bruce starts whacking at* **HARRY MORGAN**'s *hands with his 5 iron. Now it's* **HARRY MORGAN**'s *turn to scream.* **HARRY MORGAN** *lets go of Bruce's leg.*)

ROBERT BRUCE. Did you see what he just did to me!

FELICITY. I did.

ROBERT BRUCE. *What the hell's happening to the ground?*

HARRY MORGAN. IT'S OPENING, ROBERT! GOBBLE, GOBBLE!

(*Indeed, all around them, the ground is opening like so many hungry guppy mouths, each searching for anything that floats by, especially if it's named* **ROBERT BRUCE.**)

FELICITY. So *this* is what it's like…

HARRY MORGAN. SEE YOU IN HELL, ROBERT!

(*And with that,* **HARRY MORGAN** *is sucked down!*)

(*Bruce stares down into the hole in horror.*)

(**FELICITY** *quickly joins him in staring down, but unlike* **ROBERT BRUCE**, *her expression is one of amazement, not fear.*)

(*To their astonishment, the hole seals itself back up!*)

FELICITY. This is even better than I dreamed.

(*Suddenly* another *hole begins to open, very near to him.*)

ROBERT BRUCE. *Oh my God…*

(*Now more holes are opening, all reaching for him.*)

How come they don't want you?

FELICITY. Not sure.

(*Suddenly, he sees the rock.*)

ROBERT BRUCE. What's that?

FELICITY. The rock.

ROBERT BRUCE. *Thank God!*

(*He heads for the rock.*)

FELICITY. Actually, that may not be a good idea.

ROBERT BRUCE. If you've got a better one, let me have it.

(*Now he's on the rock. As if in reaction, the thunder roars in a whole new way.*)

FELICITY. I think maybe the island is angry with you!

ROBERT BRUCE. *(to the heavens)* FINE! I WON'T BUILD HERE! *Just down below.*

(*A bolt of lightning strikes the rock.*)

(*He leaps off and into one of those mouth-like holes.*)

OH MY GOD!

(*Now he's in the grip of the hole, and being sucked down.*)

FELICITY. What's it like?

ROBERT BRUCE. *(as he's sinking)* What's it *like?*

FELICITY. Yes. Being sucked into the earth like that. *Specifically.*

ROBERT BRUCE. Specifically, it's FUCKING AWFUL! Now get me out of here!

FELICITY. I think you're in too far.

ROBERT BRUCE. *Oh my God…*

(*suddenly, from the distance, we hear…*)

CHARLES. *(offstage)* FATHERRRRR…!!!!

ROBERT BRUCE. *Pearse?*

(**CHARLES** *runs on.*)

CHARLES. Do you realize who I am?

ROBERT BRUCE. *(sinking slowly as he talks)* What the hell are you talking about?

CHARLES. I am your *son!*

ROBERT BRUCE. My *son?*

CHARLES. Yes! Your *SON!*

ROBERT BRUCE. Who's the mother?

CHARLES. Sally!

ROBERT BRUCE. Sally *Who?*

CHARLES. Sally…actually I don't know her last name. In fact, she may not have had one. But she was from this island, that much I do know, and I think you knew her, you know, biblically.

ROBERT BRUCE. That girl was your *mother?*

CHARLES. Yes. By the way, I didn't know this till just now, when all at once, pow, I just saw it! It's an ability faeries have, which I obviously inherited from her, 'cause she was a faerie too.

ROBERT BRUCE. She was a faerie?

CHARLES. Yes, but in human form. Like Fiona! Who, by the way, I am going to marry. Anyway, knowing this, would you consider maybe give us your blessing? I realize this is all a bit sudden, still – *OH MY GOD! (to* **FELICITY***)* Have you seen what's *happening* here?

FELICITY. I have. Isn't it extraordinary?

CHARLES. It really is!

ROBERT BRUCE. Right. Now could you could you please get me the fuck out of here?

CHARLES. Oh. Yes. Right. Here, get up.

ROBERT BRUCE. Thank you.

(**CHARLES** *takes his father's hand.*)

CHARLES. You seem to be stuck. Felicity! Here, quick, grab my other hand!

FELICITY. No. Let him go.

ROBERT BRUCE. Let me *go?*

CHARLES. He's my FATHER!

ROBERT BRUCE. He's my SON!

FELICITY. Doesn't matter. The island wants him more.

(*Suddenly a loud sucking sound is heard, as if from a pneumatic tube, and* **ROBERT BRUCE** *is sucked under. Woosh!*)

CHARLES. Oh no… (*into the hole, a cry of anguish*) DAAAAAD?

(**CHARLES** *listens. Strnage sucking noises are heard from way below; sounds a bit like major drainage.*)

(*When those sounds are finally gone…*)

FELICITY. Well at least you had that…I never knew my dad at all, you know. Just me mum, and frankly I never much cared for her. No, you're lucky, having a moment like that…

CHARLES. Tell me this is a dream.

FELICITY. That would be lying.

(*Another hole opens, not far from* **FELICITY**, *with an odd light glowing from deep within. She drops her golf bags.*)

CHARLES. No…

FELICITY. I have to. *This is what I've lived for…*and I'm betting those Bog People felt the same. Why else would they have gone so willingly? And with those erections yet! (*she's about to jump in, when…*) Actually, now that I think of it, a little preparation might not hurt.

(*She kisses* **CHARLES**, *passionately.*)

Actually, that was rather good. You sure you don't want to come along?

CHARLES. No, thank you, I'm fine here.

FELICITY. Well, you know where to reach me.

(*And with that, she jumps in.*)

CHARLES. Oh my God…

*(Again, strange sounds are heard, only this time —
unlike **ROBERT BRUCE**'s sounds of descent, which were
distinctly carnivorous, a bit like jackals feeding — these
seem rather erotic and enjoyable, in a Hieronymus Bosch
sort of way.)*

*(The voice and specter of the **WASHERWOMAN** appear
once more in the swirls and shadows of the storm.)*

WASHERWOMAN. *(eerily)*
AND ONLY THREE
RETURN TO TOWN
SO ONE OF THEM
CAN CLAIM HIS CROWN.

THE SEA IS THE SEA AND THE EARTH 'THE EARTH
AND ALL'S MADE WELL ONCE TRUTH IS BIRTHED.

*(And with that, the storm passes, the **WASHERWOMAN**
fades from view, shafts of golden sunlight emerge from
the clouds, the ground recovers, and birds are heard.)*

(Somehow, the land has healed itself.)

*(**CHARLES** gazes around is astonishment.)*

*(In the distance, **FIONA** and **OLD ANGUS** reach the
summit.)*

FIONA. Charles?

CHARLES. Yes! Over here! *(still hardly able to believe it)* I'm all
right…

(He continues to gaze around in astonishment.)

(More birds are heard.)

(They seem to be coming in from everywhere.)

(beat)

(blackout)

*(In the dark, a projection is seen. It says: ONE YEAR
LATER.)*

Coda

(The Pub. **MACKENZIE STEWART** *stands by a table, waiting to take the order of two nervous-looking clergymen, the Right Reverend Andrew Hume, and the Right Reverend Ian Knox.* **LITTLE NICK** *is behind the bar, looking rather nervous himself. No sign of* **FIONA**, *no sign of* **CHARLES**.*)*

MACKENZIE STEWART. Ya sure I can't get you a drink while ya wait?

REVEREND KNOX. How much longer do you think that will be?

MACKENZIE STEWART. Well I can't really say. But we have sent word.

REVEREND HUME. This is all quite disturbing, as I'm sure you can imagine.

LITTLE NICK. Perhaps a drink would help!

MACKENZIE STEWART. May I suggest our single-malt?

REVEREND KNOX. Why not?

MACKENZIE STEWART. TWO SINGLE-MALTS!

LITTLE NICK. CUMMIN' UP!

MACKENZIE STEWART. And perhaps some food.

REVEREND HUME. What do you recommend?

MACKENZIE STEWART. Well the fish is good.

(Enter, the **REVEREND HAGGLEHORNE** *in filthy overalls, hair unkempt, but all-in-all looking extremely happy – though perhaps a tad nervous.)*

REVEREND HAGGLEHORNE. I'm so sorry!

REVEREND KNOX. About being late, or the condition of your church?

REVEREND HUME. *Former* church.

REVEREND HAGGLEHORNE. Well I suppose perhaps a bit o' both. Would ya mind if I cleaned up a little? I've been workin' hard as you can see, and my hands...in fact my clothes...

REVEREND KNOX. No, please.

REVEREND HUME. Anything to get rid of that smell.

REVEREND HAGGLEHORNE. It's from dealin' with all those *fish.*

REVEREND KNOX. We understand.

(*exit* **REVEREND HAGGLEHORNE**)

(*to* **REVEREND HUME**) Now that we have seen him, I would say excommunication is too kind.

REVEREND HUME. I agree.

LITTLE NICK. There ya go. Two drams of our famous single malt.

MACKENZIE STEWART. Bottoms up.

(*They each take a drink.*)

REVEREND HUME. Oh God save me!

REVEREND KNOX. *Jesu!*

LITTLE NICK. Bit on the strong side, is it?

REVEREND HUME. *I can't talk!*

REVEREND KNOX. Quick! Some water!

LITTLE NICK. Cummin' up!

(*As* **LITTLE NICK** *goes for water,* **WILLIAM ROSS** *enters, fitter than we've ever seen him.*)

MACKENZIE STEWART. Willy!

ROSS. Evenin', Mackenzie. Well-well, two men o' the cloth...

LITTLE NICK. Here's yer water.

REVEREND KNOX. Thank you.

(*One gulp does it for them both.*)

Oh my God!

REVEREND HUME. *Jesu!*

ROSS. (*while the two clergymen struggle to recover*) What brings *them* here?

MACKENZIE STEWART. Rumors. Somehow the central branch of our National Church received word that our beloved little *parish* church had been turned into a smokehouse, with dear Reverend Hagglehorne in charge o' the smokin'. And these gentlemen were sent to check it out. And have found out it is true.

ROSS. Which makes it not a rumor anymore.

REVEREND HUME. Now it's simply a disgrace!

MACKENZIE STEWART. Unless ya like smoked salmon, haddock and cod.

LITTLE NICK. Those are our specialties.

(*REVEREND HAGGLEHORNE re-enters, only slightly neater.*)

REVEREND HAGGLEHORNE. There now, a bit cleaner. Funny, you work with fish all day, ya just get this smell, which I must say I love, but I can understand why some might not.

MACKENZIE STEWART. Have ya seen Angus?

REVEREND HAGGLEHORNE. Yes, he's bringin' in the catch. And it's a good one! No surprise there. Ever since the royal weddin' the fish have been in residence like ya canno' believe. I mean stick your toe in and ya catch one. (*to the two ministers*) By the way, have ya tried our local single malt? If you've not, it's a good introduction.

REVEREND HUME. (*feeling sick*) Which way's the loo?

MACKENZIE STEWART. That way.

(*REVEREND HUME, mistaking a curtain for the entrance to the loo, pulls the curtain aside.*)

REVEREND HUME. (*loud scream*)

(*What pulling this curtain has revealed is* **FELICITY**, *transformed into a Bog Person, clad in pagan greens, huge frozen smile of ecstasy on her now leathery face.*)

MACKENZIE STEWART. Oh yes! Right. About *her...*

LITTLE NICK. Notice if ya will that the woman did die *smilin'.*

REVEREND HAGGLEHORNE. Which says somethin' hopeful about the afterlife, I would think.

MACKENZIE STEWART. Which is important to bear in mind as you turn this little incident over in your minds.

(**REVEREND HUME** *malittle desperate dash for what he thinks is the bathroom, and pulls* another *curtain aside – revealing* **ROBERT BRUCE** *as a bog person being utilized as a coat rack.*)

Now this is a different matter.

LITTLE NICK. As you can see, this man definitely did not die happy.

REVEREND HUME. Who *are* you people!?

MACKENZIE STEWART. Yes, well now that is a tricky one. Willie?

ROSS. Actually, if truth be told, we're still workin' on that ourselves.

(*Enter, from the kitchen,* **FIONA**, *proudly carrying a red-haired infant boy.* **CHARLES**, *next to her, is wearing an apron and chef's hat, vaguely resembling a crown.*)

MACKENZIE STEWART. And here they are now…

ALL. THE ROYAL COUPLE!

CHARLES. *(to the clergymen)* May I suggest the stripers?

MACKENZIE STEWART. Take 'em. He's a great chef.

(**FIONA** *spots* **ROBERT BRUCE**'s *Bog Body.*)

FIONA. Oh dear.

CHARLES. *(proudly)* That's me da!

ROSS. But "bogified."

CHARLES. He's actually much nicer like this.

MACKENZIE STEWART. And makes a helluva good coat rack, too!

REVEREND KNOX. I think the devil must be here.

MACKENZIE STEWART. No, but once upon a time he was.

CHARLES. So who here would like fish?

REVEREND HUME. We're not hungry anymore.

REVEREND KNOX. *(re the two Bog Bodies)* Do the police know about all this?

MACKENZIE STEWART. Oh yes, and they're as confused as you.

(enter **OLD ANGUS,** *carrying a humongous rack of fish)*

Angus!

OLD ANGUS. Evenin', all!

FIONA. Good catch today!

OLD ANGUS. And this is just half of it. I dropped the rest off at the smokehouse. *(seeing the clergymen) I mean church. (leaning in to the two ministers)* As usual, the Good Lord provides.

MACKENZIE STEWART. By any chance do our visiting Right Reverends play golf? 'Cause if ya do, may I suggest a round before you go. It's just a nine hole course, the gift of Mr. Willy Ross.

ALL. WILLY ROSS!

MACKENZIE STEWART. But it suits us well, and today bein' a Monday, you can play to your hearts' content.

ROSS. Unlike tomorrow, when ya really shouldn't even set foot on it.

MACKENZIE STEWART. Tell our visiting reverends how it came t' pass. (Talk about miracles!)

ROSS. Well I was on me death bed.

MACKENZIE STEWART. Which he'd been lingerin' on for many a month. And frankly we were gettin' sick of 'm.

ROSS. So one day they all come in – I'll never forget it!

MACKENZIE STEWART. "Willy," we say, "This is it, make up yer mind, die or not."

ROSS. And I thought, *there's got t' be some other choice!*

MACKENZIE STEWART. And with that, he raises up his head...

REVEREND HAGGLEHORNE. Fixes us with a gaze like the Lord Himself is within him!

OLD ANGUS. And says...

MACKENZIE STEWART. *Say it Willy.*

OLD ANGUS. Say it!

ROSS. "I do hereby deed my entire property to this fair island for use as a golf course – nine hole or eighteen, it's up to you."

MACKENZIE STEWART. Whereupon, suddenly the door opens and a gust of wind blows in –

REVEREND HAGGLEHORNE. Nearly knocks us down!

OLD ANGUS. Followed immediately by an old woman –

MACKENZIE STEWART. Holding a washboard!

OLD ANGUS. And that very shirt!

ROSS. Or one just like it.

MACKENZIE STEWART. *Fully cleaned!*

OLD ANGUS. And she hands it to him…

MACKENZIE STEWART. And without so much as a fare-thee-well, out she goes.

ROSS. And the shirt has never needed cleanin' again.

REVEREND KNOX. Well that is a really interesting story.

MACKENZIE STEWART. Fine, be skeptical. We're used t' that by now.

OLD ANGUS. Here's somethin' even better: he's not had a sick day since.

REVEREND KNOX. No, that is a truly interesting story. I must try to remember it.

MACKENZIE STEWART. But the strangest of all? Try as ya might, ya cannot lose a golf ball there.

ROSS. It's true! We try all the time!

MACKENZIE STEWART. Slice it, hook it, shank it, it don't matter: somehow yer ball just pops up.

OLD ANGUS. Almost like a hand has lifted it.

ROSS. So wha' d'ya say?

MACKENZIE STEWART. Wanna give the course a try?

REVEREND HUME. Thank you, but I think we'll pass on that.

MACKENZIE STEWART. As you wish.

OLD ANGUS. Still, ya gotta eat. My son-in-law's a fantastic chef!

LITTLE NICK. Who knew?

MACKENZIE STEWART. But he is.

FIONA. Is he ever!

OLD ANGUS. And Scottish too!

FIONA. Say somethin'.

CHARLES. *(thick Scottish accent) Whut?*

MACKENZIE STEWART. That's enough.

ROSS. *(to the clergymen)* It's just been one surprise after another.

CHARLES. If ya don't fancy fish, may I suggest the *haggis a l'orange*.

FIONA. He invented it.

MACKENZIE STEWART. It's been a huge hit. Good thing you're here today, 'cause we're booked solid tonight.

FIONA. Not just tonight.

MACKENZIE STEWART. That's right. This whole month.

OLD ANGUS. In fact we're so popular, Willy's turned his house into a bed 'n breakfast.

ROSS. *(re: the office upstairs)* I sleep upstairs now.

MACKENZIE STEWART. *(re: REVEREND HAGGLEHORNE)* Oh! And if ya ever decide t' give up the cloth, you can work for him.

REVEREND HAGGLEHORNE. In the smokehouse.

REVEREND KNOX. I really do need a drink.

MACKENZIE STEWART. Okay. A little hint. If ya just dip a finger in, and take it very gradually, one can get used to it.

(The two clergymen take his suggestion. Obviously, its still not what you'd call smooth, but at least it's possible.)

So what else would you like to know?

REVEREND KNOX. What do we tell them when we go back?

REVEREND HUME. 'Cause we have to file some kind o' report.

REVEREND KNOX. We can't just say nuthin'.

REVEREND HUME. And obviously we can't tell 'em *this.*

MACKENZIE STEWART. No, guess ya can't.

LITTLE NICK. It's a stumper.

REVEREND HAGGLEHORNE. What about *this?*

(All eyes turn to **REVEREND HAGGLEHORNE.***)*

Why don't ya just say, *"Things are goin' well."*

(The two visiting clergymen think it over. As they do, everyone else does too. Not a bad idea…)

(Then the little red-haired infant begins to cry.)

*(***FIONA** *quickly comforts him. But just to help things along…)*

(First **FIONA,** *then* **OLD ANGUS,** *then* **MACKENZIE STEWART,** *then the others, begin to sing* Sumer Is Icumen In *in round form, four-part if possible, with* **FIONA***'s amazing voice standing out.)*

(Then **CHARLES***'s less-than-amazing voice joins hers. Indeed, by now, albeit reluctantly, even the two visiting clergymen have joined in. It's wild in here. But somehow, the baby seems to like it, and calms back down.)*

(as the singing continues…)

(and the lights fade…)

(Curtain.)

Act 2, Scene 1 (translated)

The following pages contain a segment from Act Two, Scene 1, which starts on page 62 of that scene, and goes through page 64, in which a strange language is spoken by Angus and Fiona. Since what they say will be, and should be, incomprehensible to Charles, and therefore the audience, it is not translated in the script, so the reader can have the proper experience.

However, the actors will know what they're saying. Because of this, we, in the audience, will at least sense their intentions. These pages contain that odd dialogue, with those cryptic lines translated, so the reader who is curious can find out exactly what they were saying.

OLD ANGUS. Well then you're out o' your fuckin' minds.

FIONA. Glinna ei d^ol l^u. *[Something strange is going on.]*

OLD ANGUS. I agree.

FIONA. Doorst brukanni? *[He was on the rock?]*

OLD ANGUS. Brukanni! Doorst brukanni! *[The rock! He was on the rock!]*

FIONA. Basvittu! Cara d^orta! *[Well that just makes no sense.]*

OLD ANGUS. *Unglayna... [Unless...]*

FIONA. *Unglayna... [...Unless...]*

CHARLES. I'm sorry. Is that Gaelic?

OLD ANGUS. No.

FIONA. Sit up.

CHARLES. *What?*

OLD ANGUS. Sit up and lean forward.

FIONA. We need to check something.

> (**CHARLES** *does as bid.* **FIONA** *pulls out his shirt and peers down his back.*)
>
> *Look at this.*
>
> (**OLD ANGUS** *looks*)

OLD ANGUS. How long have you had this?

CHARLES. What?

FIONA. This stain.

CHARLES. What stain?

OLD ANGUS. On your left shoulder blade.

CHARLES. I don't know what you're talking about.

OLD ANGUS. Get him a mirror.

> (**FIONA** *runs, gets a mirror, runs back and holds it up behind* **CHARLES** *'s shoulder.*)

CHARLES. I've never seen it before.

FIONA. *(to her father)* Gleena deesfu-deegy. *[This is getting interesting.]*

OLD ANGUS. Su, githwynith y vaethor boe ben y d^barametta. *[Maybe we should spread salt around.]*

FIONA. Y á tirë. *[Good idea.]*

> (**FIONA** *goes to a cabinet, gets out a box of salt, and starts sprinkling salt around the perimeter of the room.*)

CHARLES. Excuse me, but what is your daughter doing?

OLD ANGUS. Sprinkling salt around the room. Nungin du-fenneltassa! *[Don't forget the windowsills.]*

FIONA. Right.

> (*She spreads salt by the windows.*)

OLD ANGUS. Un duportlenacka. *[And the door jam.]*

FIONA. I know, I know.

> (*Finished with the windows, she spreads salt by the door. As she works…*)

Marku d^ulma una peetafeern? *[What about a peat fire?]*

OLD ANGUS. Good idea.

> (*While* **FIONA** *completes her tasks,* **OLD ANGUS** *starts a peat fire.*)

CHARLES. Forgive me, but don't you think the room is warm enough as is?

OLD ANGUS. This is not for warmth.

CHARLES. Well I hope it's not for smell, because the smell is terrible.

FIONA. Actually, smell is part of it.

OLD ANGUS. There! What next?

FIONA. P^inji, hithu gwann ma th^unga banya. *[I think maybe we should give him a bath.]*

OLD ANGUS. Ahhh! Yo. Welsa! Modo-welsa! *[Good thinking.]* (*to* **CHARLES**) We have decided the time has come for you to take a bath.

CHARLES. …really!

FIONA. So if you don't mind, would you please take your clothes off?

CHARLES. …ummm, here?

OLD ANGUS. Here, or where the bath is, it doesn't really matter.

www.ingramcontent.com/pod-product-compliance
Lightning Source LLC
Chambersburg PA
CBHW070625120726

47909CB00004B/1332